WRAPPED IN DANGER

*World War II Gifts Surface
With Perilous Consequences*

By

BARBARA W. TEAL

Brilliant Books Literary
137 Forest Park Lane Thomasville
North Carolina 27360 USA

I would like to dedicate, the book, Wrapped In Danger to the Golden Retrievers of the world who like Toby, the Retriever character in the book, are not just super in hunting and retrieving but also in sniffing out clues, and particularly, if trained in protection, can help to solve mysteries.

This dedication also goes to my late Golden Retriever, Quincy.

Acknowledgement

Wrapped in Danger acknowledges and honors all the Americans and our Allies who fought and served in World War II including those civilians who worked for the war effort both in the United States and abroad.

CHAPTER I

1944, World War II, Holland

As the story goes, after one of the hottest summers ever experienced in Holland, a group of Dutch farmers were working in the green fields and orchards adjoining the Dutch village of Mesch. They and most of the population of Holland were weary and always fearful after four years of Nazi control. Would they be the next to be killed? So, one could imagine how startled and gripped with fear they were by a strange noise, and looking around were shocked to see that they had been surrounded by soldiers. They froze. More startling was that one of these uniformed men with a cigarette hanging from his mouth even had a grin flashing across his face. The soldier called out to the farmers, "You are liberated. The Allies are here!"

The group of farmers were facing the soldiers of the U.S. Army's 30th Infantry Division. The soldiers tried to explain to the farmers, hoping they could understand some English, that they were there as part of America's support in freeing Holland from the clutches of Nazi control.

The soldiers had no idea of what still lay ahead. The small country of Holland was flat with few places to hide. The Nazis were vicious.

With the help of the 82nd Airborne Division, the Americans tried to secure the many bridges, and were successful except for the last bridge over Arnhem, thus their operations had failed.

Two hundred sixty soldiers had been killed. Months of intense fighting followed.

CHAPTER 2

Winter of 1945, Holland

Captain Sam, as he was called, walked through the Army camp to the hospital tent. All he could think about was how strong his soldiers were. They had endured such fierce fighting while also battling the intense cold of a winter which seemed to be as unforgiving as the enemy. He knew that American military training was the best. Most military training traditionally stressed the importance of the buddy system. In basic training, especially, GI's were taught to subordinate their own concerns to the good of the group which they were serving—their squad, their platoon and the Army or Marine Corps. He had heard that there was at least one US psychiatrist who had argued that hate for an enemy may serve as a soldier's "steel helmet for the mind", thus making him less vulnerable to the stress of killing and also of seeing his buddies die.

The Captain always visited the hospital tent every night. On this particular night, he had heard there were more serious injuries than usual.

Entering the tent, he quietly went from cot to cot saying a few words of encouragement to his men and sometimes sharing a prayer with them. As he approached the last cot, he could see the serious injuries of this particular soldier. He bent down and in a low gentle voice looked at his name tag which also included his religion and said: "Joey, this is Captain Sam. I hope the nurses are keeping you comfortable. Is there anything I can get for you?"

Joey could barely open his eyes. He slowly pointed to his pocket. The Captain touched the pocket, then slid his hand in and pulled out a folded paper.

"Is this what you want, Joey?"

Joey slowly nodded and whispered in a barely audible voice, "Please mail this to the address on the outside. The note holds important information for my family. It's very important and urgent. It is about the protection of their livelihood"

The Captain checked the address. The address was a small town in Michigan. The soldier answered:

"Yes, it's for my my parents from their parents who said they were fleeing Germany for the United States. They sent some of their important valuables on ahead. My parents need to know where to look for them."

Sadness engulfed the Captain as he answered, "Don't worry, Joey, I'll get your letter on one of our first ships leaving for the United States. And I will follow up to see if they received it."

Joey seemed to relax and thanked the Captain, then closed his eyes as he had no more energy.

Capt. Sam patted his shoulder and told Joey, he would visit him tomorrow. As the Captain walked back to his tent, he could still hear the fierce fighting in the distance, and saw the sky light up with missiles shooting straight into the sky then turning and raining down on their targets. Capt. Sam understood Joey's urgency to get the note to his parents. He hoped Joey's grandparents had made it, but he knew that it was very difficult and dangerous for Jewish people to attempt to leave. The Captain's unit had other Jewish soldiers like Joey and Capt. Sam was very watchful that there would never be prejudice in his unit.

The following evening, the Captain went back to the hospital tent. Joey's cot was empty and the nurses informed him that Joey had passed away that morning.

The Captain immediately went back to make arrangements to send this very valuable note home to Joey's parents, and to let the military know to alert the soldiers who would visit his parents house to inform them of their son's death and that he had sent them an important message, and that they should watch their mail for it. They would also be informed of the number they could call if they had questions about when to expect it. Capt. Sam also knew that some of the Great Lakes freighters served in World War II, and hopefully he could arrange to have the note sent via the freighters as it might get to Michigan, where his family lived, in a shorter amount of time.

A few weeks later, a turning point in the war came. On February 23, 1945 when the American Forces launched 'Operation Veritable.' With the water level on the River Revel falling enough so the soldiers could cross, the Americans met the English and Canadian troops and liberated Holland from the Nazis. The Germans surrendered in Limburg.

CHAPTER 3

Present Time: Shipwreck Coast., Michigan on Lake Superior

Glenn Pedersen, a retired CEO of a marketing firm in Duluth, Minnesota, peered out the window of his hunting lodge. He could see the dark clouds quickly forming over Lake Superior and the winds whipping the waves into a white cap frenzy. His golden retriever and hunting companion, Toby, was at his side. Toby had been nervous and agitated for the last hour. Glenn knew that dogs normally sense the pressure of a storm arriving before humans take notice.

Glenn's very comfortable and deluxe hunting lodge was located in front of a pine tree forest with an expansive lawn that extended down to the top of a cliff which fell to the beach below. An old abandoned lighthouse sat on the top of the cliff. Even though there hadn't been a lighthouse keeper for years, the light still worked since it was the Coast Guard's responsibility to regularly check and service the light. Glenn had heard that the lighthouse was on a list to be auctioned off in the near future and hoped whoever bought it would remodel it as it was an eyesore. When Glenn's small grandchildren came from Duluth to visit, they would always want him to take them to the top of the cliff to peek into the lower windows of the lighthouse.

He smiled to himself thinking about how he loved to read and make up stories for his grandchildren and would always start with, "It was a dark and stormy night." This would have been the perfect night for the story. As he watched the storm approach, he noticed that there was what looked like a flashlight inside the lighthouse as if someone were walking up the spiral staircase that led to the light. The light seemed to flash through each window until it got to the top.

As Glenn grabbed his raincoat and flashlight, he looked at Toby.

"Come on, boy, let's see what's going on at the lighthouse before the rain starts to fall."

As they walked through the dark, the wind had strengthened and was hitting them head on as it came off the lake. Toby ran in front of Glenn. With the roar of the wind, the flashes of lightning and the cracking of thunder, there was no way that Glenn could have heard or sensed a person dressed in a dark parka with a hood sneaking up behind him. As the figure closed in on Glenn, he raised his arm and with the object he was carrying smashed it on Glenn's head. Falling to the ground unconscious, the attacker didn't notice Toby running back to Glenn, but as soon as he heard Toby's barking, the figure quickly disappeared into the night.

Toby was frantic running back and forth around Glenn, then nudging him with his nose and licking his face. Toby finally stood over Glenn's body to protect him. The rain began and grew to a tropical force pounding onto the ground. The cold water hitting Glenn's face slowly woke him up. Putting his hand to his head and sitting up, an excited Toby started licking his face.

"What happened, Toby? Did a tree branch get me?"

Slowly rising to his feet and with Toby by his side, they walked slowly back to the lodge to get some ice for Glenn's head. He then spent the rest of the night sitting by the fireplace, sipping brandy. He would go out the next morning to see if he could find what hit him.

The morning dawned as a clear sunny day. Glenn and Toby walked all the way to the lighthouse and back but found no evidence of a branch or any other object which could have hit his head. Only Toby knew the truth.

CHAPTER 4

The Auction House, Duluth, Minnesota

A March snowstorm had coated the streets and trees of Duluth. Even so, it hadn't dampened the enthusiasm of those arriving at the Duluth International Auction House. Someone had wiped the snow off the sign just in front of the entrance door, so it could proclaim its invitation to the quarterly lighthouse auction.

The three lighthouses which were to be auctioned off were considered excess government properties. Under the National Historic Lighthouse Preservation Act of 2000, the aging lighthouses were those rejected by eligible government agencies or nonprofit groups. So, the General Services Administration (GSA) of the federal government would auction them to the public for personal use as long as the buyer could meet certain conditions which are unique to each property. Some of those participating in the auction had visited the sites before the auction. The auction house opened two hours before the auction so the public could preview photos and read the detailed information about each property. As the potential buyers finished viewing the pictures and information of each lighthouse they registered with the auctioneer then were given a Bidder's card. Among the guests was Madeline Kirkpatrick, an innkeeper from Sault St. Marie Michigan. During the tourist season, her Twin Sisters Inn was a very popular place to stay. Especially with its nautical decorations and homey atmosphere. Its location in town was only a short walk to the world famous Soo Locks. Maddie had decided to increase her holdings, and had discovered a lighthouse situated on the top of a cliff overlooking Lake Superior. If she won it at the auction, her plan was to turn it into a Bed and Breakfast. She knew there would be a lot of remodeling and perhaps some rebuilding of the Innkeeper's house to be large enough to accommodate five bedrooms plus a living room and dining area. Because the property was situated off the 'Shipwreck Coast,' it sat against the stunning backdrop of Lake Superior with its glorious sunrises and sunsets. Boat lovers could sit for hours watching freighters from all over the world sail by. It would also be near to and accessible to popular tourist sites.

When the room filled with excited people, after they had reviewed the lighthouses and the two hours had ended, the Auctioneer stepped up to the stand and rang his bell traditionally marking the beginning of the auction.

"Good Morning, Ladies and Gentlemen, welcome to the first quarterly lighthouse auction of this year. The General Services Administration or GSA, as we call it, will be auctioning off three lighthouses this morning. You have been given a copy of the rules. If you win a bid and buy the lighthouse, you will need to have insurance on the property, and if your lighthouse has a platform, you will have to lease the platform from the Army Corps of Engineers. You will also need to agree to allow the Coast Guard in on occasion to check its navigation equipment. The Coast Guard is also responsible for the light so it will also need to check the light in order to make sure it is in good working condition. So, let's begin.

The first lighthouse is situated on Lake Michigan. Your information sheet will have the directions to this property from the closest city. You will need a boat to get to the lighthouse. The light sits above the lightkeeper's house and is attached to the roof. The bidding will begin at $ 10000.00

Immediately, bidders began yelling out their bids with their bidding cards held up high. The highest bid was $ 60000.00 which closed out the bidding. The winner of the bid went over to a side table to have his credentials and credit checked.

The second lighthouse went up for the bid. It was located off Lake Superior in the northern part of Minnesota. It stood alone on a beach with a small lightkeeper's house next to the tower. Both the house and tower appeared to need major remodeling and repairs. Again, the auction began at $ 10000.00. The bidding began. Since the auction was taking place in Duluth, most of the bidders were from Minnesota, so this property was very popular. Bidders went higher and higher until topping at $ 100,000.00 with one final winning bid of $ 105000.00 which ended the bidding.

The auctioneer called for a ten minute break so bidders could use the restrooms and stretch their legs.

As Maddie saw the bidders return, she noticed a man sitting behind her and to her right. She hadn't bid on the first two lighthouses, and she realized he hadn't either, but he had a number so must be planning on bidding on the third and last lighthouse. She assumed he would be her competitor and bid on the third lighthouse too. As she glanced at him, he appeared to be very agitated. His dark eyes looked angry.

Again the bell rang signaling the end of the break.

"Ladies and Gentlemen, the bidding will now begin for the third and last lighthouse we have today. If you didn't get the lighthouse you wanted today, our next lighthouse auction will be in June. So, let the bidding begin."

"The third lighthouse is located on the historical Shipwreck Coast over looking Lake Superior. The property is located in the state of Michigan. The lightkeeper's house is small and needs repairing. And, remember again, the Coast Guard is in charge of the light. The bidding will begin at $ 12000.00. The man behind Maddie immediately bid $ 12500.00 followed by Maddie bidding at $ 13000.00. The man bid $ 14000.00. The bidding continued on and on with others placing their bids until it was up to $100000. Maddie and the man were the final bidders with one bidding over the other. The man glared at Maddie, but she continued on holding her bid card high and bid $ 150000.00. Then the man had a coughing attack and couldn't raise his bid card. He couldn't control his coughing and it lasted just long enough so the auctioneer finally had to call Maddie's bid for $ 150000.00 as the winning bid.

The angry man jumped up and cried "that's not fair!" The auctioneer said he was sorry but he took too long of a time and he wasn't holding his bidding card up plus no one else was bidding so he had to close the bidding.

Chills went down Maddie's spine. Could the man be be so angry that he could be dangerous? She went over to the table to show her credentials and pay for her lighthouse. She paid for it in full without taking a mortgage. She would finance later if need be.

The auction house gave her a wrapped gift. When she unwrapped the gift, there was a little toy lighthouse and when she opened the door, the keys to her real lighthouse and lightkeeper's house were inside.

As she left the auction house, Maddie looked around to see if the angry man was nearby. Fortunately, he had left in a huff. She wondered why someone could become so angry over losing since there would be more lighthouse auctions.

CHAPTER 5

After the auction, Maddie took a cab directly to the Duluth Airport. She treated herself to a delicious lunch and pondered what her next move would be. She had a two hour wait for her flight back to Sault Ste. Marie. After lunch and browsing in a few gift shops, she walked to her gate.

The plane was a small aircraft since it was a short flight from Duluth to Sault Ste. Marie. There were only two seats on each side of the aisle with a ceiling so low that most men had to bend over as they walked down the aisle. She had been assigned the last seat in the back of the plane, so she took the window seat hoping she could have both seats to herself. But no such luck. A young girl appearing to be of college age or in her twenties had been assigned to the seat next to hers. She smiled and put her carry on bag in the very small upper compartment, then sat down and buckled her seat belt.

Maddie smiled and asked, "Are you going to Superior University in Sault Ste. Marie?"

The girl answered, "No I'm not at this time. I'm going to find a job."

Maddie noticed the girl had an accent and did not speak English that well. Hesitating for a minute, then asking, "I've noticed your accent and can't place it. What country are you from?" The girl said she was from Holland. So, Maddie continued, "What type of job are you looking for?" The girl responded, "I don't know. I guess anything I can find. Do you know of someone in Sault Ste. Marie who is looking for help?"

Maddie mentioned that the University might need secretarial help or help in their libraries.

"You know Sault Ste Marie is a very small town, but we have a few nice restaurants and a wonderful bookstore that sells new and used books, and even native crafts in the back of the store. The manager is very kind. There's also a beautiful old hotel in town which has a restaurant. They may need waitresses. I've just bought a lighthouse and may need help.

Where are you staying tonight?" The girl shrugged her shoulders. "I don't know."

So, Maddie continued, "Are you going to rent a car? There are other hotels outside of town like the Holiday Inn and other chains, but you would definitely need a car."

The girl looked dismayed. "I don't drive, and even if I did, I don't have an international drivers license."

Feeling sorry for the girl, Maddie decided to introduce herself. "I'm Maddie Kirkpatrick and I own the Twin Sisters Inn in Sault Ste. Marie. What's your name?"

She answered, "And I am Heidi Nilsen."

"Well, Heidi, why don't you come with me to my Inn and I can help you sort it out tomorrow and show you around town. I won't charge you."

Heidi's eyes lit up. "Thank you so much. I'd love that."

====== **CHAPTER 6** ======

Maddie was at the front desk when Heidi appeared looking for the breakfast room.

"Heidi, I hope you slept well last night. If you go up the stairs to the balcony take the first left down the hall and follow the signs to the breakfast room. When you finish, just come back and we'll talk about opportunities in Sault Ste. Marie."

Maddie noticed Heidi had a cell phone and was about to make a call as she acknowledged Maddie's instructions. The innkeeper wondered who she knew in the area to call. Heidi hadn't hinted that she knew anyone in town or had any friends or family in the United States.

After a half hour or so, Heidi returned. "You have a lovely breakfast room. The different stations have such a variety of food. I love the way your chef makes the fried eggs and the bacon was so crisp, just the way I like it."

"Why thank you Heidi. We try out best. Now follow me to my office and we can talk about where you can go from here."

As Heidi settled on a small couch facing Maddie's desk, Maddie opened her notebook and began with questions about Heidi's background.

"So, you grew up in Holland. Are your parents still living there?"

Heidi answered that they were but were nearing retirement. Maddie learned that Heidi was twenty years old and after school had a few years of working small jobs in her parents' town.

"What brought you to the United States Heidi?"

She answered that she wanted to improve her English speaking ability. Maddie told her that she had met other girls who had come to the area from other countries for that same purpose. She had understood from them that there are campgrounds in the area where they worked during the tourist season when the weather was warmer. Since most of the tourists are from the United States and Canada they do get a lot of practice speaking English. However, most of the campgrounds were across the bridge in Canada and a couple of hours away from any town so were quite isolated, but were also beautiful and very clean.

"Heidi, if you do that, the campgrounds should be opening soon. Since you don't have a car you might consider working right here at the Twin Sisters Inn. You could rotate between the front desk and working in the restaurant as a server depending on what we need. I also have a small bedroom and bath on the ground floor in the back of the inn which you could use. I am going to need help right now on both the day and night shifts since I'll be occupied with the planning and remodeling of my new lighthouse B&B so will be hiring contractors and traveling back and forth to its location on the Shipwreck Coast. So, you will get your own room with breakfast and dinner included. Lunch will be on your own and you will get a small salary. Would you be interested?"

Heidi's face lit up. "I would love that and I think I would feel safer here."

"Great, then you pack your suitcases and I'll move you to the little bedroom and after you settle in, I'll introduce you to some of the other employees and your training will begin. We'll start with the front desk."

After Heidi had moved to her room, which was tastefully decorated with the nautical theme that continued throughout the inn, and had unpacked her suitcases, Maddie introduced her to Matt, the front desk manager who would become her trainer and supervisor.

Chapter 7

As Maddie walked down the street towards the large bookstore in town, she thought about how fast things change and what a coincidence that she sat next to Heidi on the plane. A feeling of relief came over her that she was now free to come and go in order to work on her new project, the Lighthouse B&B. She would also promote Matt to Assistant Manager.

Entering the bookstore, she was surprised to hear an angry man loudly arguing with Ben, the owner. This was very unusual as everyone in town loved Ben, and he would always try his best to accommodate their needs. As she glanced over, she gasped. The man making the commotion was the angry man from the auction who lost the bid on the lighthouse to her.

"What's he doing in town, she thought" Trying to avoid him, she immediately went to the back of the store where Native American crafts were displayed with other gift items. The bookstore was the biggest store in town and also a central meet up place for the town people.

The arguing continued so she moved closer to the front in case Ben needed help. Finally, the man threw up his hands and turned to leave. As he did so, he glanced towards Maddie and instantly recognized her. In a threatening voice, he yelled, "It's you who stole the lighthouse from me. You're going to pay for that!!"

Moving forward Maddie answered in a controlled voice, "Sir, I bought that lighthouse fair and square at the auction and you know it. Why don't you take your anger outside and stop bothering these people!"

He slammed the door on his way out. Maddie turned to Ben, "What was his problem?"

"I don't know, Maddie. I've never seen him before. He's not from around here but wanted information on treasures found in this area. I guided him to some books but he didn't get what he wanted. So, did I hear you say you just bought a lighthouse? Congratulations!"

"Yes, Ben, I did at the Duluth auction a couple of days ago and he wanted the one I got but it didn't work in his favor. He was very angry there and stomped out of the auction in a heat of rage."

"I hope, Maddie, he doesn't stay in town. Now, what can I help you with?"

Maddie asked him if he had information about the Shipwreck Coast with its history and nearby tourist attractions. Maddie also said she was looking for hunting lodges in that area so she could contact the owners to ask for references for contractors and builders in or near the Shipwreck Coast.

Ben, who was the town expert in Michigan's upper peninsula, led her to several books. As she paid for her armful of materials, she could see that Ben, who had been so shaken by the angry man, was back to his mild mannered self.

"Thank you Ben. I'll keep you in the loop and up to date on the lighthouse since you're such an expert in this area. Hope that guy doesn't come back to bug you. If he does, I wouldn't hesitate to call the police."

＝ ＝ ＝ ＝ **CHAPTER 8** ＝ ＝ ＝ ＝

Back in her office, Maddie first looked through the material to find some contacts at the Shipwreck Coast area. That part of the Upper Peninsula was about an hour drive from Sault Ste Marie so would have to find a place to stay close by the lighthouse to check on the progress and to work out the usual problems that normally arise in the process of remodeling. But, first, she would have to hire an architect to design her B&B.

She had seen a beautiful big hunting lodge very close to her lighthouse and would try to find the name of the owner to phone him or maybe she should knock on his door.

Maddie's first reference would be Ben since he knew more people in the Sault Ste. Marie area and even across the bridge to Canada in Sault. Ste. Marie, Ontario. An immediate return to the bookstore tomorrow would jump start her research and she could even check to see if the angry man had returned. Angry people like that rarely, if ever, showed up in the little town of Sault Ste. Marie, but for some reason she had a nagging feeling about him.

The next morning Maddie made an early visit to the bookstore.

"Hi, Ben, I'm back. Hope you've recovered from that incident with that obnoxious man yesterday."

"Hey, Maddie, glad you asked. Fortunately, he hasn't returned. Hopefully, he has left town. So, what can I do for you?"

Maddie told Ben that since she was planning the restoring and remodeling of the lighthouse, she was wondering if he could refer her to building contractors especially anyone who has had experience working on lighthouses. She told him that she would ask Bob Wilkins, the architect in town, if his firm would work with her. "And one more thing, do you have a list of people who own hunting lodges in the area of the Shipwreck Coast. There is a beautiful one behind the lighthouse and I will definitely contact the owner."

Fortunately, the bookstore had no customers in the store yet due to the early morning hour, so Ben had time to check for builders in the area and gave Maddie the list, then commented, "Looking at this list, Maddie, the construction company I would recommend is Elstad Construction Group. I've seen their work and I think they have done work on lighthouses. Their main office is in Duluth, but their group also has an office in Sault Ste. Marie, Ontario, Canada just across the bridge. Their office is over there because they have a lot of Canadian accounts and I have been told it is less expensive to have an office in Canada.

As for the lodge owners, I know of the one near your lighthouse who probably is the one you referenced and his name is Glenn Pedersen. I've met him once and I can get his phone number for you in a minute."

Maddie thanked Ben and decided to check with Bob Wilkins office on the way back to the inn. Bob was the only architect in town and was known throughout the upper peninsula. As she approached his building, she marveled at its sleek modern design. It was close enough to Ben's bookstore that she could walk. The building was located down by the St. Mary's River front with magnificent views of the Soo Locks, the St. Mary's River, and the constant freighter activity.

Approaching the reception desk she asked if Bob were available for a short appointment. Everyone in the office knew Maddie.

"Mr. Wilkins is in but he has someone with him, but I will buzz him and tell him your here. Since he is also a friend, I'm sure he will see you for a few minutes."

The receptionist was right and after a few minutes, ushered her into Bob Wilkins' office.

"I haven't seen you in a while, Maddie. How's everything at the inn? Although I'm getting curious, I only have a few minutes"

After explaining her mission, Bob suggested she take pictures of the lighthouse and yard and make a list of her ideas then make an appointment and he would arrange to see her right away.

Thanking him, and feeling as if her project had begun, she started the long walk back to the inn. As she approached the inn's front door, it flew open and the angry man who had been at Ben's bookstore came charging out. He didn't look her way but turned in the opposite direction. Maddie was shaken and hurried in. Heidi was at the front desk.

"What did that man want, Heidi? He seemed almost combatant. "I know Maddie. He wanted a room, but I said we were full. We really aren't, but I was scared of him."

"You did the right thing, Heidi. Does Matt know?"

"Yes, but he was in the back room and didn't see it."

"Just to let you know, Heidi, that man was at Ben's bookstore when I was there and was verbally attacking Ben. I had seen that man at the auction in Duluth, and he confronted me saying the lighthouse should have gone to him. We should all be on the lookout for him and stay clear of him. I hope he has left town for good."

In her office and before she started drawing up her plans for the lighthouse, Maddie decided to call Glenn Pedersen. "That's a good Norwegian name. He must be from Duluth since it was settled by Norwegians a century ago."

The phone rang a few times before Glenn answered.

"Hello Glenn, my name is Maddie Kirkpatrick. I own the Twin Sisters Inn in Sault Ste. Marie, Michigan, and wanted to talk to you since your hunting lodge is near the old lighthouse which I recently bought at the Duluth auction in March."

Glenn chuckled then replied, "So you're the mystery woman I've been hearing about. I hope you have some great plans for it."

Maddie answered that she was working on the plans but first wanted to make an appointment with him to talk about the area. She told him she was driving up the next day and hoped they could meet. She also needed to take photos of the lighthouse, the keeper's house, and all the property around the house including the view of Lake Superior from the lighthouse.

She also invited him to see the inside of the lighthouse with her.

Glenn was happy to oblige and to meet a seemingly remarkable entrepreneurial woman who was taking on quite a project.

"I will be here, Maddie, all week. Why don't you first come to my lodge, we can meet, have some lunch then go down to the lighthouse. Do you have my address and are you familiar with the roads?"

Maddie told him she had the directions and would call him when she was a short distance from the lodge.

= = = = **CHAPTER 9** = = = =

Maddie Kirkpatrick was excited and full of anticipation as she headed out of town to see her lighthouse for the first time since her purchase. She was eager to meet her new neighbor, Glenn Pedersen. As she drove the country roads to Munising, Michigan where she would stay, she found it hard to keep her eyes on her driving due to the stunning scenery of sand stone cliffs, water falls and even inland lakes. When the drive began through Hiawatha National Forest, since it was still March, the trees were still without leaves. In the fall, however, the sugar maple trees and red Maples plus the American BeechTrees put on such a breathtaking show of spectacular color, Maddie knew her B&B would be sold out from September to December.

Reaching Munising, she checked into her hotel for a two night stay, then headed out to Glenn's lodge and to the lighthouse.

As she approached Glenn's lodge, she could see her lighthouse in the distance on the top of the cliff overlooking Lake Superior. Steering her car into Glenn's driveway, she marveled at how handsome and inviting the lodge appeared. She rang his doorbell, and Glenn immediately opened the door.

"You must be Maddie Kirkpatrick. Welcome."

"It is so nice to meet you, Glenn, or should I say 'neighbor.' Thanks for seeing me on such short notice. And who is this lovely companion at your side. He's a Golden Retriever, my favorite dog."

Glenn introduced Toby who was wriggling with excitement, but had been trained very well not to jump on guests.

"Can I get you something to drink, Maddie?"

"I would love a warm cup of tea if that's not too much trouble."

Glenn returned with two cups of tea, a plate of lemon slices, a vegetable platter with dip, and some cheese and crackers, and some cookies.

"I thought you would like a small lunch since it is past noon."

"This will be just perfect, Glenn. I haven't had much to eat today."

As she drank her tea and enjoyed the snacks, she asked Glenn, how long he had lived in the lodge. He explained that he had built the lodge before retiring from his job as a CEO for a marketing firm in Duluth. In the warm weather, he and his late wife would flee from the tensions and busyness of the city for long weekends just to unwind. His grown children and grandchildren would come for summer vacation.

"My whole family loves the outdoors so we do a lot of hiking in Hiawatha National Forest, and visiting the plethora of tourist spots which are nearby. I even have a deal with one of the nicest hotels in Munising to allow my grandkids to swim in their outdoor pool in the summer since it is too dangerous and cold to swim in Lake Superior. The hotel manager is my hunting buddy so in return when we go hunting, I let his friends stay at the lodge for free."

"I thought you were retired here."

"I am. This has become my home, but I do own a condo in Duluth since I'm still involved as a consultant with my former company and need to attend various meetings."

Changing the subject back to Maddie, Glenn inquired, "I've heard wonderful reviews and testimonials about your Twin Sisters Inn in Sault Ste Marie, so what do you have planned for the lighthouse?"

"I have decided to turn it into a B&B and know that a lot of renovation both to the lighthouse and to the light keeper's house will be needed. This is the reason I bought it during the March auction in Duluth since it will give me time to submit my designs and start the work, hopefully in the next couple of months so we can make some progress before next winter sets in. I'm hoping the work can continue to December before stopping until the March thaw.

Glenn smiled and added: "It is pretty rough up here in the winter months, but I've been through it and you can count on me to check on your project and report back to you if anything is amiss."

Then, Glenn remarked on what happened the night before and turned to Maddie, "I need to tell you of a strange experience I had the other night. A storm was brewing over Lake Superior and coming our way. I was watching the approaching storm. It was late in the afternoon so it was already dark. I saw a flashlight coming through the lighthouse windows and it moved from window to window as if someone were in there and walking up the stairs to the top. Toby and I walked across the lawn to check it out, and before we got there something bashed my head and I fell unconscious. Toby stayed with me standing over me to protect me. Obviously, he was very anxious. When the rain began, the cold water on my face woke me up. After I stumbled back to the lodge with Toby, except for being shaken up and a sore bump on my head, I was okay. When Toby and I went back in the morning to see if we could find anything like a tree branch that could have hit me, there was nothing, just a few twigs lying around. So, my question to you is does anyone else have a key to your property?"

Maddie shook her head and knew of no one.

"Glenn, I am so sorry but when I get back to Sault Ste. Marie, I'll make arrangements to have the lock changed."

"But, Maddie, we have a locksmith here in Munising who is very good and honest. I have used him. So, why don't you do that before you leave?"

"Thank you, Glenn, I can't believe I didn't think of that. I will need to orient my thinking to the local businesses around here and perhaps later you can help me with other contacts."

As dusk was settling in and it would soon be dark, Glenn, Maddie and Toby began the trek to the lighthouse. As they neared the top of the cliff where the lighthouse stood, Maddie tightened her knit scarf around her neck against the biting cold of the wind and lake. The waves were whipping into a frenzy.

Maddie's key unlocked the door with ease and they stepped inside to find a steep winding spiral stair case reaching up to the top level which was just beneath the light. The lighthouse light was turned on even though the lighthouse had been abandoned for a few years. The Coast Guard had to continue servicing the light.

Maddie and Glenn beamed their flashlights up the stairwell.

"I think I am going to wait until the morning to walk on up. If you are going to be here tomorrow, Glenn, you are welcome to come with me."

As they walked back to the lodge, Maddie decided to return to her hotel and told Glenn she would contact the locksmith in the morning before coming back.

"There's only one locksmith in town, Maddie, and he is centrally located, so I'll let the hotel direct you. If you need my help, Toby and I will be here. See you in the morning."

Maddie patted Toby goodby and went to her car. Hopefully she would have the time to start on preliminary plans for what she wanted as a design for the lighthouse and light keeper's house before retiring for the night. But first, she was determined to have dinner not only to eat but to check out restaurants in Munising. She would have to learn about the town and surrounding areas so she could guide her guests as they vacationed on the ShipWreck Coast. There were so many attractions and areas with rich history and heritage, one could not see everything in one visit. Hopefully this would build repeat customers and the word would get around. In addition, she decided to rely heavily on Glenn to teach her about hunting so that in the off season she would be familiar with hunters' routines, the rules for hunting, and where to get hunting licenses and more.

She liked and trusted Glenn. He would definitely be her hunting consultant and hopefully could get the word around that her B&B is open to the hunting groups.

Arriving in Munising, Maddie drove slowly down Main Street mindfully taking inventory of the variety of small restaurants and eateries. She chose a small restaurant with curtains in the windows and a cozy glow coming from the dining area, probably from a fire place.

Asking for a table for one, the host escorted her to a corner table in front of a large fireplace in full flame emitting a wonderful fragrance of firewood. Looking at the menu, Maddie knew immediately what she would order.

"Have you made your choice, Madame?"

The waiter was an older balding man who looked like he had spent his life at the restaurant. Change came slowly to the Upper Peninsula, but with it came a comfortable homey feeling.

"I have," Maddie answered. "I have decided on one of my favorites, a Pasty, and I know that Pasties are the adopted, unofficial State dish.

Did you know that in 1968 Governor George Romney declared May 24 the official statewide Michigan Pasty Day?"

The waiter laughed. "We all know that around here. So, what do you want in your Pasty. Will you choose to start with the traditional potato and onion base and sometimes rutabaga?"

In looking at the options on the menu, Maddie chose in addition to the traditional base, chicken, zucchini, carrots and broccoli. "And I will also have a glass of Merlot, please."

After the waiter left, Maddie glanced at the brochure wedged between the napkin holder and the salt and pepper shakers. Appropriately, the title was "The History of the Pasty." She always loved to review its ancient history.

The Pasty could be traced back from 1150 to 1190. They were even mentioned in Robin Hood ballads of the 1300's. The Pasties were brought by the Cornish from England to the Upper Peninsula when they came to work in the copper mines. Back then, it was the standard lunch for the miners. Today we would call it 'a pot pie' since it consists of pie dough in a sort of diamond shape. The ingredients of meat, vegetables, potatoes and onion or whatever one wanted was rolled up in the dough. Then, the ends were pressed together just like a cook would press the top and bottom of the dough to enclose the inside filling of a pie. These types of sandwiches served as the miner's lunch and would stay warm from their home oven for at least six hours. Since entire Cornish families would work in the mines and each member wanted separate ingredients, the Cornish wife would stamp the bottom corner of each pasty with an initial so to personalize each pasty.

At this point in her reading, Maddie was interrupted by the waiter. "I forgot to ask you, Madame, for your initials so we can imprint them on one end of the pasty's crust. We try to be very authentic here."

"They are "MK", she answered. She then turned back to her reading. While sipping her wine, she noticed a small latticed wall separating the dining room from another area. She thought it probably was a small dining area for special groups. The area behind the wall was dark. As she gazed at it, a sudden chill moved down her spine as a strong feeling came over her that someone was watching her, but she could not see any movement.

Before she could finish her reading, the waiter returned with her steaming pasty and a garden salad.

"Would you like another glass of Merlot, Madame?"

"Thank you, that would be very nice."

The waiter continued, "Now, do you know the traditional way of eating these pasties is to hold the pasty in your hand and begin to bite it at the opposite end from where the initial is. And not to scare you, but in the days when the tin mines were open the crimped crusty edge of the pie was just as important as the filling. For safety's sake a miner could hold the whole pie by the crust and start eating in the middle, then toss the edges aside. It wasn't that they were picky, but in working with tin, their hands were contaminated with arsenic. So, the crust kept them from contaminating their food with whatever arsenic would be on their hands. There was no way of washing their hands when they were down in the mines. Of course this doesn't happen today and I can assure you of complete safety."

Maddie looked startled. "I have never heard of that, but it does make sense."

The waiter continued, "the children are always interested in this story because, as legend has it, small goblins hang out in the mines, and when the miner had finished his lunch and thrown the crust aside, the 'buccas' or small goblins, would eat the crust which would make them happy so they saw that any accidents would be avoided keeping the miners safe."

Maddie laughed, "I guess the arsenic didn't affect the goblins."

The waiter replied, "Probably not, but the legend doesn't mention that. Hope you enjoy your meal. Please let me know if you need anything else."

Arriving back at the hotel Maddie phoned Matt to check on the inn and was happy that all was going smoothly and that Heidi had fit in so quickly. The customers liked her.

Tomorrow, after contacting the locksmith, she and Glenn would do a thorough inspection of the lighthouse and Keeper's house.

CHAPTER 10

At 10:00 AM Glenn's doorbell rang. Toby immediately barked and crossed excitedly and swiftly to welcome the guest. Putting his hand on Toby's head to quiet him, Glenn opened the door knowing it was Maddie.

"Come on in Maddie." I'm looking forward to our inspection of your property, and afterwards I hope you will have lunch with me." Do you mind if Toby comes with us to the lighthouse? Once he knows who our guest is, he'll calm down."

"No problem, Glenn, so let's go." It's quite chilly outside and I'm sure the lighthouse won't be any warmer. We'll check the lighthouse first then I want to see what shape the Keeper's house is in."

As they trudged across the large expansive lawn towards Lake Superior, the wind seemed to rip at their faces. Maddie tightened her warm winter scarf around her neck and pushed the front part up under her nose.. Glenn looked over at her.

"I would have thought you'd be used to this lake weather. Is this worse than in Sault Ste. Marie?"

"Yes, it is, Glenn. Remember, we are not directly on the lake as the locks are closer to the St. Mary's River, but it is still very cold."

As they entered the lighthouse, since it stood near the top of a cliff leading down to the beach below, the wind whistling around the windows lent an eerie and spooky feel to the whole atmosphere. As Maddie stood there listening, she asked Glenn what he thought of the wind.

"I haven't thought about it much because I have that sound around my lodge when there is a storm. It is spooky though. When my grandkids are here during a storm, it's hard for them to sleep at night."

"More than spooky, Glenn, the wind sounds like human voices or cries of anguish. I hope it doesn't frighten the guests. I hope they don't think this place is haunted."

"You will get used to it and so will they. You might warn them about it upon check-in."

As they climbed the spiral stairs in order to start their inspection at the top, it took a lot of effort and Maddie immediately wondered if a designer architect could modify the climb or perhaps it would be possible to put in an elevator. Finally, when they reached the top, Maddie discovered that the lighthouse was not only a beacon for the freighters and other ships, but could also be turned into a vantage point from which guests could take in the breathtaking views of the lake with its ships from around the world. She felt as though she could see almost down to Sault Ste. Marie. She hoped she could turn the circle of space, which had a security railing around it into a patio in the sky with attractive lounge chairs and tables so during the summer guests could grab a few rays of sun while drinking in the scenery. The circle of space was under the lighthouse light so it would be fun sitting on the patio watching as the light beams moved across the water.

As they descended the spiral staircase slowly, Maddie noticed the cracks in the wall that would need repair. Every once in a while she also saw a few cubby holes. Perhaps, they could be used to display decorative lanterns or special lights to lend a less spooky atmosphere. As they descended further, there were more ledges, and she was surprised to see small bags with crumbled paper sticking out the top as if they were carry out meal bags from a drive-thru such as Arbys or MacDonalds. They didn't appear to have been there for a longtime.

"Glenn, look at these carryout food bags. Someone has been in here recently. Maybe there was a person here the night you saw the flashlights in the windows. Someone must have a key."

"Have you contacted the locksmith yet?"

"Yes, I did before leaving this morning. He said he'll try to make it over here as soon as possible."

When they got to the ground floor, Maddie saw that there was enough space for a lounge area. She immediately started imagining how attractive and cozy it could be with the proper design. As she walked around the base of the lighthouse, on the side facing the lake, crumbled up against the inner wall was a blanket. Partially wrapped in the blanket were tools of the type one would use to pry doors or anything open as if searching for something.

Again, Maddie pointed that out to Glenn.

"What could possibly be in this lighthouse that anyone would want or were searching for? Now more than ever we need to see if anything is going on in the Keeper's house next door and I have a different key for that house."

Maddie had great hopes for the Keeper's house since that would be the main B&B with bedrooms, dining space and lounges both inside and on an outside porch.

Approaching the house, Maddie and Glenn were surprised that it still appeared to be well preserved since it hadn't been lived in for some years. She opened the door and saw chaos with trash strewn all over. The foyer was large and as she and Glenn checked the dining area and the five bedrooms upstairs, they were impressed with the size of the bedrooms and the possibilities of a total remodeling plan with little renovation needed.

Each bedroom had a fireplace with some of the bedrooms looking towards Lake Superior. The house was heated with a gas water heater and the electricity could be turned on with little repair. "Glenn, the trash in this house doesn't look that old. How could someone had gotten in here. It almost looks like someone has been living here, but there are no broken windows or locks. Hopefully, that locksmith can get here tomorrow."

Toby, who had been quite calm during their tour of the house was becoming agitated as he sniffed around. Glenn bent down, "What's wrong, Toby? Why are you so nervous?"

Toby whined, and became more nervous as if he were on the trail of something.

"Maybe, Glenn, there's food spoiled on the floor. Let's go look at the kitchen."

Toby followed them into the kitchen. There was a gas stove, a medium sized refrigerator and an old fashioned sink with no disposal. The linoleum floor needed to be replaced and Maddie knew the kitchen would have to be renovated to commercial grade and to a standard so it could pass inspection for them to be able to serve guests.

Maddie opened the refrigerator door and drew back in horror. The pungent smell of the rotting food almost made her gag. She slammed the door.

"This whole refrigerator is going to the dump."

"Well, Maddie, it looks like someone's been using this house as their residence. I still can't figure out how they got in."

"Glenn is there a basement in this house or is it on a slab?"

"Maddie, houses out here usually have basements so let's see where the door is. I saw a hatchway door on the outside so there must be two entrances and exits."

The first door they opened was a pantry, then they saw a door just outside the entrance to the kitchen. They slowly opened the door and found the stairs to the basement.

"Be careful, Maddie, we don't know what shape these stairs are in."

Shining his flashlight down the stairs, Glenn thought they looked fairly sturdy. Grasping the handrail, he cautiously stepped on the first step. Very gingerly and carefully he put his foot on each step until he reached the bottom. Looking up at Maddie he cautioned, "Be careful, but I think it's okay to come down."

Maddie was as cautious and careful as Glenn. Since the electricity hadn't be turned on to the house, they both directed their flashlights around the basement space. Half the floor was dirt and the other had a cheap piece of linoleum over the dirt.

Toby stood in the doorway above and whined. He refused to go down the stairs as if he felt danger.

"So, Glenn, what do you think Toby knows that we don't know? Is he usually like this?"

"Not, really, but you know that dogs have a heightened sense of feeling danger, and of feeling vibrations around them just like they can feel when a storm is coming on before we know there is one approaching the area. Toby is my barometer."

Toby started barking and nervously moving back and forth at the top of the stairs. Something was wrong. However, Glenn and Maddie continued flashing the lights around the room and every corner. Under the stairway was the typical open space. The type that most people would put in drywall around it making it a closet under the stairs. Glenn then shined his light into the open space under the stairs. In the far back and barely noticeable was an old fashioned wardrobe trunk from probably the 1920's. It was very difficult to see so it was barely noticeable against the stairs.

"I've found something, Maddie, let's pull it out of here. I don't have gloves so I hope I don't get bitten by something like a brown recluse spider. They like to hide in basements and dark places."

Toby started barking hysterically as if to warn them.

"I'll stay here with Toby, Glenn. Maybe he'll calm down, and you can go get the gloves. I don't want you to take the risk."

"Okay, Maddie, I'm going to grab a camping lantern too which will make it easier to see in this dark basement."

As soon as they reached the top of the stairs, Toby calmed down, so Glenn left for his lodge.

With Toby close to her side, he followed Maddie around the main floor as she looked at the walls, windows, fireplaces, and into as many corners she could find. She still had the feeling that someone was using the house for some reason and whoever it was knew of her plans to renovate.

A half hour passed before Glenn returned with the lantern and some leather gloves. He had also brought a smaller pair of gloves for Maddie. As they descended into the dark of the basement, Maddie felt as if she were returning to a dungeon. Toby remained upstairs in the doorway.

Back under the stairs, Maddie held the lantern high. Both flashlights were pointing towards the trunk. As Glenn approached, he picked up one flashlight and closely inspected the outside of the trunk. He ran his gloved hand over the trunk as if dusting it off. He saw no spiders. There was a handle on both sides of the trunk. Since it was an old wardrobe trunk, it stood up vertically with a door that would open like a closet and usually there would be hangers attached to a rod and drawers for lingerie, underwear, sweaters and so on.

"You take one side, Maddie, and I'll take the other. We'll pull it out from under the stairs and drag it over to the bottom of the stairs. We won't be able to take it upstairs so open it down here unless it is locked."

After quite an effort, both positioned the heavy wardrobe trunk at the bottom of the stairs. Toby stood at the top of the stairs staring down at the spectacle below. Glenn checked around the trunk for a key. Laying the trunk on its side, he checked its bottom.

"We're lucky, Maddie, there is a key taped to the bottom of the trunk."

First, they had to stand the trunk back up. The key did fit the lock, and he unlocked the door.

As he slowly opened the door, he asked Maddie to hold the lantern as high as she could. What they saw was a wardrobe out of the previous century. There were womens' dresses and nightgowns. Opening the drawers, they found old jewelry which appeared to be cheap costume jewelry, and then some high topped womens' shoes. As they pushed the hanging clothes aside, they gasped. Hardly believing what they saw when Maddie held the lantern as close as she could. Behind the clothes was the skeleton of an adult human female person. She was dressed in a faded white lacy floor length gown, a style out of the early 1900's.

Collecting his thoughts, Glenn looked at Maddie, "I can't believe this. Who would have done such a thing? We're going to call the police immediately, and the coroner and medical examiner will have to be notified."

They slowly closed the door to the wardrobe trunk and locked it. Glenn took the key.

"Let's get out of here."

A half hour later, the police arrived with no sirens followed by the Coroners truck. After looking at the skeleton and contents of the trunk, the Coroner decided they should take the whole wardrobe trunk into his office in Munising and transfer it to the Medical Examiner's lab. Then, addressing Maddie and Glenn, he said, "I'm going to test all the contents of the trunk and try to date them. The skeleton will probably be very fragile so I'll treat it very carefully and will be able to tell you something about it in a few days. In the meantime, you should try to get some information on the former residents of the house going back as far as you can. The property court or library might be the first place to begin if they have information or could direct you to the proper place."

As Maddie and Glenn walked back across the lawn, both were deep in thought about where they should start the search.

"Glenn, do you think the local library would have records of the lightkeeper's house going back to the late 1800's and early 1900's?

"They may, Maddie, but the GSA may have historical records showing the identity of former lightkeepers. I'll check with them and will show you how to get to the library in Munising. They may have old newspaper stories which could reveal what might have happened. But, first let's get something to eat before we part ways to do our own research. There's a popular cafe in town which you will probably enjoy.

CHAPTER 11

"Thanks for the delightful lunch, Glenn. I'll call you to let you know what information I find at the library."

As Maddie entered the library, she immediately went over to the librarians' counter and asked too see the head librarian. Mrs. Espy, an older lady with tightly curled grey hair, approached the counter. "Can I help you with anything?"

Maddie introduced herself and recounted the story of the old lighthouse.

"So you're the new owner of the lighthouse? Congratulations! That's going to be quite a job remodeling it, but I'm sure our town will be enthusiastic to have a new B&B here.

Mrs. Espy led Maddie to the research area where she could scan newspapers going back to and including the 1800's. "We have quite a complete research library for such a small town. So, take as long as you want and let me know if I can be of further assistance."

Maddie decided to begin her search on one of the library's computers then use the microfiche reader for more detailed accounts printed in old newspaper stories. She googled "lighthouse keeper stories 1890 to 1910." Several stories popped up about how lighthouse keeping was not for the faint hearted. The keepers had to live in isolation although some had their families with them. They had to endure violent storms and had to respond to the occasional ship wreck. In addition, they had to be self sufficient, handy with tools and maintenance, and comfortable with heights. If a keeper's family had children, and if their lighthouse was located off land, the mother was in charge of rowing her children to the mainland where they would attend the closest school. The keeper's car would be parked on the mainland. The wives of the keepers also assisted in water rescues. As Maddie continued reading, a clue seemed to jump out of the print and caught her attention. Since one of the major responsibilities of the lightkeeper was to ensure that the light's massive lens kept spinning all day and everyday, and in the 1890's some keepers began floating their lenses in liquid mercury because in the liquid mercury the lens's metal base spun more easily thus helping the light to rotate faster with less frequent winding by the keeper. The result was a quicker flash which was safer for the seafarers, but not for the light keeper who touched and breathed the mercury on their daily cleaning rounds. Thus, scholars have wondered if the exposure to mercury more than the isolation of their job was behind reports of some of them behaving erratically or losing their sanity since chronic exposure to mercury poisoning usually caused confusion, depression and hallucinations. The articles even mentioned that one lighthouse keeper had been committed to an insane asylum because of his violent behavior towards his wife.

Maddie immediately moved over to the microfiche machine then scanned back to the newspapers of the 1890's to 1905. Excitement grew as she came upon an article from 1904. The picture showed a lighthouse on the Shipwreck Coast near Munising, Michigan. It was her lighthouse. The headline read "Lighthouse Keeper and Wife Disappear." As she scrolled down the article, it mentioned that even though it was considered the town's gossip, there was a belief that the keeper had become violent towards his wife. Only a few people in town had talked to the wife when she came to town for groceries. Unlike most keepers' families, they stayed to themselves. After a few weeks of not having contact with them, a few of the town's leaders went to see if they were okay. They found the lighthouse and keeper's house empty and no one seemed to be anywhere on the property. Thinking the couple may have taken a trip to visit family, they left then returned a few days later. Still there was no family on the grounds.

The lighthouse light was still working. Finally, the town council, who had a spare key to the property returned to enter the keeper's house and the lighthouse. No one was there.

Maddie continued to scan the following newspapers for any updated articles on the case. Finally, the story continued in the newspaper a few weeks later. An article reported that the body of the lighthouse keeper was found about a half mile away in some thick shrubs at the top of the cliff. It appeared that he had shot himself. Suicide was not uncommon among a small percentage of lighthouse keepers. But, still his wife had not been found, and after a few weeks the search ended. The police deemed the case a murder-suicide.

Maddie found it strange that no one had discovered the old wardrobe trunk in the house. She figured the skeleton that she had found was that of the wife. Hopefully, the coroner's report would verify that. She was determined more then ever to remodel the house. Perhaps she would have it torn down. A new house would have none of these memories even though the history of the property would have to mention this incident over a hundred years ago. There were already many stories about the dark and mysterious sides of other keepers' houses and their lighthouses on or near the Shipwreck Coast. Mixed in were also the stories of more than three hundred ships that sank to their graveyard at the bottom of Lake Superior during the last century and beyond. The cemetery on the lake's bottom held many skeletons and possible treasures tweaking one's imagination and leading to numerous ghost stories and supernatural sightings.

Maddie immediately phoned Glenn with her findings.

"You found a great clue, Maddie. I phoned the department of the General Services Administration that handles the lighthouses. They may have a list of retired light keepers. We need to find out why none of the other residents found that trunk in the keeper's house."

"There's nothing more we can do Glenn until we get the medical examiner's report on the skeleton. Until then, I'm calling my architect to begin some designs for the property."

CHAPTER 12

Back at the Twin Sisters Inn and with a briefcase full of photos of the keeper's house and the lighthouse including the surrounding property, Maddie phoned Bob Wilkins, the architect, to make an appointment. She was given an appointment for that afternoon. Then, checking with Matt and Heidi who assured her that all was running smoothly at the inn, she left for the privacy of her office to take notes on her ideas for designing the remodeling which she would share with Bob Wilkins.

That afternoon as soon as she had settled into the reception area of the architect's office, Bob Wilkins immediately appeared in the reception area to greet her.

"Hello, Maddie. I am so happy to be working with you. Your lighthouse project is so exciting. "So, let's go to my office so I can hear your ideas."

After showing Bob her photos, then sharing the story of the skeleton, he could see that through all of her excitement, the skeleton incident had caused some anxiety and hesitancy.

"Maddie, I don't want the skeleton incident to dampen your enthusiasm, but I don't think you should demolish the keeper's house but to expand it which will definitely feel new to you. At least the facade should replicate its history and the architecture and design of the century in which it was built. The inside can be modernized with an open and welcoming design. We can also design some small bedrooms in the lighthouse but will have to check on availability of plumbing, water and electricity."

"Bob, why don't you come back with me for a day to get a feel of the place. I have to be back tomorrow to let the locksmith in."

"I can be there the day after tomorrow then we won't have to work around the locksmith. And, one more thing. Have you chosen a contractor for the remodeling?"

Maddie mentioned that she had been referred to Elstad Construction.

"They're a good group, Maddie, and they have remodeled old lighthouses. Tell them you are working with me. They will give you great service and will promptly deliver what is promised."

On the way back to the Twin Sisters Inn, a surge of confidence blew away her anxiety. She knew she could trust Bob Wilkins and also his recommendation of Elstad Construction. She preferred to work with people from her hometown of Sault Ste. Marie. She was also looking forward to spending the night at the inn before returning to the hotel in Munising the next morning.

CHAPTER 13

CHAPTER 13

As Maddie checked back into the hotel in Munising, she began to feel at home in the little town and was determined to meet the merchants as soon as possible, but would first check in with Glenn.

Fortunately, where Glenn's house and the lighthouse were located, the road to Glenn's driveway was white gravel, then passing his house, the gravel road curved slightly to the right and led to the keeper's house and lighthouse at the top of the cliff. Her first thought was the need for a small parking lot in front of the keeper's house.

Glenn was playing fetch with Toby in his front yard. Toby was a very astute dog chasing the ball across the vast stretch of lawn almost to the lighthouse before retrieving it and returning to Glenn. Noticing Maddie's arrival, Glenn signaled to Toby to return to the front porch.

"Looks like you and Toby are having a lot of fun."

"Hey, Maddie, we are. It's just our daily exercise. Toby has the run of this place and has never gotten lost. I'm sure if I ever get lost he'll find me, and he likes you too so will watch over you too."

Toby came over to greet Maddie and she patted his side.

"If you have the time, Glenn, I have some questions about the utilities around here."

"Okay, then let's go inside to have some coffee or tea, and I'll fill you in about how all that works around here."

Settling in to one of his comfy chairs, Maddie listened as he described how since their location was so close to the town of Munising, the town was able to extend the pipe lines to his house and was able to hook into the town's electricity. He also explained that her keeper's house and the lighthouse could also hook into those pipes which might have to be extended down to her place.

"However, Maddie, you already have a gas water heater and gas stove in the keeper's house which probably is less expensive than electric heat especially around here with the long cold winters we have. And you really don't need air conditioning much in the summer time. There are also generators that could be used, if needed. The contractor you hire should know about this and will be responsible for getting the required inspection."

"Oh, I forgot to tell you that last night I saw some lights coming from inside the lighthouse again, then a few minutes later I saw them flashing around from inside the keeper's house. I wasn't about to check it out this time because of what happened before."

"Well, Glenn, the locksmith is coming today so hopefully it won't continue. Someone must have a key, but, why would they be there and what are they looking for? This is getting spooky."

The doorbell rang and Maddie and Glenn were startled to see how early the locksmith had arrived. He explained that his previous appointment was shorter than he thought. Maddie led the locksmith to the keeper's house first. She had borrowed a broom and dust pan from Glenn and decided to clean up as the locksmith worked.

After inspecting the locks, the locksmith turned to Maddie, "Ms. Kirkpatrick, these locks are ancient. I suggest we replace the whole lock system rather than just making new keys."

"How ancient do you think they are?"

Thinking for a moment, he replied, "At least forty to fifty years old. Anyone could have easily picked them."

Maddie explained how her neighbor had seen flashes of light shinning around the inside of the house just the night before and was wondering if someone was spending nights there.

"Do you have any homeless or transients in this area," she asked.

"Not that I know of. Our little town doesn't have homeless on the streets. We have shelters for those who need help"

As Maddie began to sweep up the trash, her mind turned back to the wardrobe trunk. Something around the property wasn't right. She had a horrible feeling that there was something bigger going on then she could imagine. Maddie looked up as she heard Toby's bark.

Glenn and Toby were crossing the lawn to the keeper's house.

"Just wanted to see how it's going and to let you know I received a call from the lighthouse section of the GSA. I have the name of the former light keeper. It has been at least ten years and the guy is retired and living near here. I didn't realize this lighthouse had been abandoned for that long probably because I never saw him and he had no family. The light lens on the lighthouse was always working. I always saw the coast guard coming to inspect it but I never saw him."

"Do you have his phone number, Glenn?"

"Yes, and I have his address, so if you're finished with your sweeping, we can go back and call him to see if we could pay him a visit."

Maddie checked with the locksmith who said he wouldn't be finished until the evening which would give them enough time to visit the former light keeper then return before the locksmith went home.

Glenn offered to phone the man for Maddie. The former light keeper, Mr. Fiske, immediately invited them over, happy to have company.

Mr. Fiske's house was on the edge of town going towards Sault Ste. Marie. He was a man in his seventies with thick grey hair. He enthusiastically invited them in and led them to his small but cozy living room. He brought in some pretzels in a small dish and took their drink orders. "Would you like a beer or a soda?" Both Maddie and Glenn opted for a soda. After serving them their drinks, Mr. Fiske sat opposite them with a curious expression and asked, "Are you the new owners of the lighthouse and keeper's house?"

"I am," Maddie answered. "I will be remodeling both the lighthouse and keeper's house to use them as a bed and breakfast. I figure there will be a big tourist market in the summer, than in the winter, it would be open to hunters."

"So, how can I help you?" Mr. Fiske asked.

"Both Glenn and I have been checking around the property and found a wardrobe trunk in the basement of the house. So, my question is, do you know who that belonged to. Was it in the basement when you lived there?"

"I really didn't go into the basement much when I lived there. I don't remember seeing a trunk. Where was it located in the basement?"

"Underneath the stairwell," Maddie replied. So, Mr. Fiske continued, "I'm sure I didn't see it. Is there a problem with it?"

Maddie and Glenn glanced at each other then responded, "Yes, and it's very mysterious. We found a key taped to the bottom of the trunk, and when we opened it, there were some very old clothes belonging to a woman. The clothes appeared to be almost one hundred years old. But that's not all. The clothes were hanging on a closet rod and when we pushed them to the side, there was an old vintage dress wedged in the back on the floor clothing a skeleton.

Mr. Fiske reacted immediately. "Oh my God, how could something like that have gotten there. I can't imagine. I lived there over ten years and never saw it. I was the only one in the house and wasn't even married."

Maddie asked, "Did you ever meet the lightkeeper who lived there before you took over the job?"

"No, Ms. Kirkpatrick. When I accepted the job, the GSA sent me the keys to the keeper's house and the lighthouse. However, I remember getting the feeling that he had quit unexpectedly."

Maddie and Glenn explained that the medical examiner in town was examining the skeleton and would get back to them.

"I hope this doesn't put a damper on your plans, Ms. Kirkpatrick. Our town will enthusiastically welcome your B&B."

Maddie and Glenn thanked Mr. Fiske for his graciousness, and said they needed to get back to talk to the locksmith who was rebuilding all the locks. Mr. Fiske thanked them for informing him about the happenings at the keeper's house.

"I am sure this will be in the local newspaper. This is a small town and stories like this travel fast."

Chapter 14

The locksmith was sitting in his car finishing the paperwork as Glenn's car pulled up next to his. Glenn invited him into the lodge so they could review the invoice and Maddie could give him his check.

"Here are three sets of keys, Ms. Kirkpatrick, for both the keeper's house and the lighthouse.

I think you'll like the style of lock. The locks are attractive and they go with the era of the house and lighthouse. It's very simple. Just put the key in and turn. If you have a problem please let me know. I would also suggest you consider putting in a security system for each building. I'm also affiliated with a security company in town so let us know when you are ready."

Maddie handed him a check and he gave her a receipt and an information booklet describing the lock system. As the locksmith left and backed his car out to head towards the road, he had to drive over grass to pass the Sheriff's jeep which was approaching the house.

Glenn greeted the Sheriff at the door.

"Is Ms. Kirkpatrick here?"

Maddie crossed the room. "I'm here Sheriff. Do you have any news for us?"

"We should sit down, Ms. Kirkpatrick, since this will take a few minutes to explain." Then, the Sheriff explained that he had called in one of the area's best forensic anthropologists. The first thing the forensic guy would determine would be to see if the skeletal remains are human. He had determined that the remains were human. Then he looked at the bones to determine age and gender, then the age at time of death and the overall age. To do this, the Sheriff explained that they use a method called Carbon-14 testing which is used all over the world. The forensic guy had also told the Sheriff that the most important way to determine gender was to look at the width of the pelvis. Since the female body is designed for childbirth, her pelvis is wider and longer than a male and has a rounder pelvic inlet. So, then the Sheriff announced that this was the case with the skeleton, so they felt sure the skeleton was a female.

Then, the Sheriff hesitated to sip his water, and continued.

"Then he tried to figure the age of the woman. To do that he looked at the wear and tear of the bones which start at age twenty five. The older the person gets, the more cracks are in the bones and the cartilage would be worn down. By age thirty one's bones are still growing and the ends of the shafts are fusing to short bone caps, but these caps fuse at different stages of growth. By looking at these, an accurate age can be determined. Therefore, he could tell that this skeleton, a woman, was probably in her late thirties due to the percentage of degeneration in her bones. Another sign of probable age is the skull. The squiggly lines on the skull were barely noticeable which meant an age approaching forty. And one more thing, this woman had given birth to a child since there were small pock marks on the inside of the pelvic bone which are caused by the ligaments tearing during childbirth. But you can't tell how many times she gave birth to a child only that childbirth had occurred."

The Sheriff asked Maddie and Glenn if they had found any information regarding previous light keepers. They related the information they had learned from Mr. Fiske.

"But Sheriff, Mr. Fiske had lived in the keeper's house for ten years and said he had never seen a trunk under the stairwell. He lived there alone, and as far as we know, he was the last lighthouse keeper to live there."

Maddie continued that Mr. Fiske had heard that the light keeper before him had been married and had left unexpectedly.

The Sheriff said he would try to identify the light keeper serving before Mr. Fiske and if he had descendants.

"Ms. Kirkpatrick, my office will keep the trunk and skeleton until we complete the investigation. In the meantime, you continue with your plans."

He turned to go then stopped and looked back at Maddie to ask:

"Do you think someone planted that trunk there to scare you? Do you know anyone who wouldn't have wanted you to take possession of that property?"

"Sheriff, the only one I can think of is a man who was at the Duluth auction house and he bid on the same property. He was very angry when he didn't get the bid, and I won the property. He was even in Sault Ste. Marie shortly after the auction and actually went into my inn when I wasn't there. My employee at the front desk was frightened by the gruff way he approached her, so she did not rent a room to him."

"I'll remember that Ms. Kirkpatrick. Let me know if you see him around town. Good Day."

CHAPTER 15

Bob Wilkins had left a phone message for Maddie that he planned on driving out to the Shipwreck Coast in the morning and would be there around 10 am at the lighthouse.

After a restless night at the hotel, dreaming of skeletons, and images of the angry man appearing, then disappearing, she awoke to a warm sunny room which seemed to melt away the nightmares. The hotel's breakfast of bacon, eggs, fresh fruit, sweet rolls and coffee hit the spot. It was served in a small parlor room lending to a feeling of being with family during morning breakfast.

Driving over to the lighthouse, she stopped first at Glenn's house to let him know she would be waiting for the architect to meet her in front of the lighthouse, but first she wanted to check the locks at the keeper's house. She unlocked the door with ease. There was nothing stiff about the new lock. Its gleaming gold facade was quite decorative, and once the front door was repainted, she would have quite a handsome entrance to her keeper's house. The same was true for the door to the lighthouse.

Exactly on the hour of 10 am she heard the crushing of gravel as Bob's car approached the parking area in front of the keeper's house. She ran up to greet him at the parking lot.

"This is a beautiful location, Maddie. We'll have a lot of fun remodeling the property."

"Why don't you come into the keeper's house and leave your briefcase and other work files inside. That way we can walk around the property so you can see it from different angles and take pictures."

It was a breezy cold but sunny day. Bob was meticulously checking out every corner, curve and window of the exterior. Both he and Maddie ascended the one hundred fifty steps to the Gallery Deck which would be open to tourists for viewing Lake Superior and its surroundings for miles. Most of the time Bob was silent as he took photos from all angles. On the way down from the Gallery Deck, they stopped at the landings. Maddie could tell he was trying to figure out where to put the bedrooms. Finally, reaching the bottom of the lighthouse, Bob looked at Maddie to suggest his ideas.

"I have a lot of information here, and I already have some thoughts about what we should do. Maddie, you have a prize here. We'll make this into something fabulous. But, first, while I go back to my office to draw up the designs, you need to contact Elstad Construction to invite their team to tour the property. Then we'll all meet at my office in Sault Ste. Marie to go over the design and their plans. This way you can meet the construction crew who will be here for the next several months creating your B&B."

CHAPTER 16

"Hello, you've reached Elstad Construction. How may I direct your call?"

Maddie responded, "This is Maddie Kirkpatrick calling. Could I please speak to Brad Estad?"

"Why, Maddie Kirkpatrick, it is such a pleasure to talk to our town's favorite innkeeper."

"I'm so glad you like my Twin Sisters Inn, Brad, and now I have another inn on the Shipwreck Coast. I would love for your team to help me remodel it. But, first, I'd like to take you on a tour around the property. It's quite unique since it is a lighthouse."

"Wow, Maddie, this should be fun. Does it have ghosts?"

"Only a skeleton, Brad, and that's not a joke."

"What are you talking about?"

Then, Maddie explained about the wardrobe trunk in the basement of the keeper's house and finding the skeleton inside.

"The Medical Examiner is still researching the skeleton with clothing and other odds and ends found in the trunk."

She assured him that everything was safe. Brad suggested that he would drive up at lunchtime and bring a couple of his men with him.

At the stroke of noon, Brad's red pickup rolled up to the parking lot in front of the keeper's house. Maddie waved to him from the front door as he and his men came walking towards her.

"Hey, Maddie, this is a beautiful property. I'd like you to meet my team who will be working on the property. Brad turned to a man who appeared to be in his early thirties and introduced him as Greg. Then turned to a younger man.

"Maddie, this is my nephew, Wilson Joseph Hall."

"Glad to meet you Wilson", Maddie replied as she shook Wilson's hand.

"Thank you, Ms Kirkpatrick, but please call me 'Wil' as all my family and friends do."

"So, Wil, you have such a strong name."

"Ms. Kirkpatrick, I'm named after a family member. Wilson or Wil is from my mom's side, and Joseph is after a cousin who fought in World War II and was our hero. He was called Joey, and died in the war. Even when he was injured he was able to arrange for some very important information to be delivered to our family in America which they needed for their livelihood back then."

"That's a great story, Wil. You must be so proud. My great grandfather was also a World War two hero. He was a Captain and as the story has been passed down through the generations, he was close to his men and always watched out for them."

Maddie immediately felt a bond with Wil.

"So, how long have you been in the construction business, Wil?"

"Ms. Kirkpatrick, I'm presently a college student and am taking what we call a 'gap year,' which means we take a year off from classes to get some business training. My majors are criminal justice and art history, but I love to work with my hands and along side Uncle Brad."

"Well, welcome to the business world, Wil."

Maddie proceeded to show them around the property and through the light house and keeper's house.

"So Maddie," Brad asked, "Are you going to be the lighthouse keeper or continue to stay in Sault Ste. Marie?"

"I haven't figured that out yet, Brad, but know I'll need a lot of help."

After a couple of hours checking out the properties, Brad told Maddie he and his team would love to help her with the construction and remodeling of the two properties. She informed Brad that they would be working with Bob Wilkins from Sault Ste. Marie as the architect and they all would need to meet at his office.

"That's great, Maddie." As you probably know, our office is in Canada so is very near the inn.

I've worked with Bob before and will call him to advise him that my team will be working with you."

As the men bid goodbye, Maddie felt relieved that she was working with such honest people. As their truck pulled away, she had no idea that there was another car behind a blind of bushes with a passenger watching her every move.

She was surprised to find a message from Matt, her assistant manager of the Twin Sisters Inn. His message asked her to phone him as soon as possible upon her return to the hotel.

"Hi Matt, what's going on."

"Maddie, everything is okay here, but just wanted to let you know that Heidi has been going to lunch and disappearing for two or three hours at a time. She knows she only has an hour for lunch, but when I remind her, she blows it off with excuses. I don't know where she would be going in our little town that would take that long."

"Thanks, Matt. I'm returning tomorrow and we both can figure this out when I finish with my meeting."

CHAPTER 17

Bob Wilkins welcomed Maddie Kirkpatrick and Brad Elstad, owner of Elstad Construction to his architectural firm in Sault Ste. Marie. He then presented Maddie and Brad with a diagram of the lighthouse. From the lightning rod on the top down to the foundation, he had labeled every part of the lighthouse and defined each part's function. Then he pointed out the areas in the lighthouse which would be open to tourists.

There was the Lantern Room which housed the light. Bob reminded them that the Coast Guard will be in charge of servicing the light. They would make an appointment to come into the lighthouse. Beneath the light was a catwalk and a widow's walk which would be off limits to tourists. The first available tourist deck would be the Gallery Deck beneath the widow's walk then, there were the windows up and down and opposite the spiral stairwell that led from the ground floor to the Gallery Deck.

Every few feet there was a ledge where people could leave the stairs and look out through a window. Bob proposed that at some of these ledges he might be able to expand them into a few small bedrooms. He explained that this had been done in other lighthouses, but, of course, most of the B&B bedrooms would be in the keeper's house along with a beautiful dining area with floor to ceiling windows overlooking Lake Superior.

Bob also thought that because of the long harsh winters, both the lighthouse and keeper's house would have generators supplying sufficient heat. Eventually, electricity and plumbing pipes would be extended past Glenn's lodge to the lighthouse and keeper's house.

Bob then added, "One very important issue we should consider is to make the lighthouse and keeper's house compliant with the ADA (American Disabilities Act). Since I am expecting the lighthouse to attract many senior citizens who are retired, I suggest putting in a small elevator to take them to the Gallery Deck. There are very few lighthouses in this country with elevators so your lighthouse would be unique. The lighthouse with an elevator should be advertised in your brochure or marketing materials, and would attract many more tourists. Then, finally we will improve the spiral staircase but still keep it authentic looking. So, what do you think about these ideas, Maddie?"

"I think this is a fantastic start and I know, Brad, you will make this happen for me, and I hope your nephew, Wil, will have a large part in this too."

"Don't worry, Maddie, all of us are ready to take on this project. I'm glad we're starting now since it is springtime and we'll have decent weather for the next six months. After that, we'll work on the inside and whatever we can do on the outside. We're not going to stop because of the harsh winter."

Maddie assured them that they would all have new keys to both houses the next day. She explained that she suspected someone had been able to get into both properties.

Brad spoke up, "Don't worry Maddie, our eyes are open to this, and won't let anyone into you property while we work on it and double check every evening that both houses are sufficiently locked before we leave. We are there for you."

Chapter 18

"Good Morning, Heidi. When you have the chance, will you please come over to my office.

We have a few things to talk about."

After a few minutes, there was a knock on Maddie's door.

"Hi Heidi, just take a seat. I wanted to talk to you about how you are enjoying your job and if there is any assistance you need."

"I'm good, Maddie. I've had to take some long lunches and I hope Matt isn't too upset with me."

"Oh, is anything wrong, Heidi?"

"Not really. It's just that sometimes I need to be alone."

"Well, Heidi, I can understand that but as an employee, you really need to stick to the rules and that is everyone only gets an hour for lunch. Anything longer is not fair to Matt. So, can I count on you to keep your break no longer than an hour?"

"Yes, Maddie I will."

Chapter 19

The first part of the construction included cleaning up the debris in the rooms. Brad had organized his team and assigned each member a job.

Maddie had purposely stayed away from the construction sight for two weeks so not to be in the way of the workers. As she pulled in front of Glenn's house, she noticed the Sheriff's car following her. He pulled in beside her.

"I have some news for you, Ms. Kirkpatrick regarding the skeleton case and was hoping you would be here. I phoned Mr. Pedersen and he told me he had spoken to you and knew you'd be over this morning."

Settling into one of Glenn's oversized chairs, the Sheriff took out the Medical Examiner's report.

"I doubled checked the story, Ms. Kirkpatrick, about the light keeper who had committed suicide out here on top of the cliff back in the early nineteen hundreds. It is true. They never found his wife's body. I have in this paper the Medical Examiner's report that verifies that the skeleton matches the size of the woman who was his wife. There was also evidence of pressure around the neck, so the Medical Examiner thinks he strangled his wife, then dressed her in what he thought was her favorite dress which was the tradition back then. He put her in the wardrobe trunk with her jewelry and probably some of her favorite clothes thinking that this would honor her. I've seen quite a few murder suicides in my career. And one more thing, he also was very controlling since he convinced her not to socialize with women in town thus isolating her."

Maddie asked, "What about the question of how the wardrobe trunk got into the keeper's house. It had to have been in other locations since there were many keepers over the past one hundred years and no one reported it."

"That's still a mystery. However, I also noticed the trunk doesn't seem that old. There aren't many scratches on it and it was very clean inside. I think it may have been moved here, and maybe that trunk didn't exist back then. Perhaps he put her body somewhere else. Since no previous keepers at the house reported it in the last century, someone could have set up that scene. This theory could also coincide with what I asked Ms. Kirkpatrick a few weeks ago if you thought anyone was trying to scare you from taking over the property.

Then there is one more historical fact. Since you found the key to the trunk scotch taped to the bottom someone could have opened it anytime in the last few years. But remember scotch tape wasn't even invented until 1930 by a 3M engineer named Richard Drew. It was the world's first transparent adhesive tape. Another bit of trivia is that Richard Drew was quite a banjo player. You can learn a lot of trivia when looking for clues."

"So, Sheriff," Glenn asked, "Doesn't that prove that someone placed the trunk in the keeper's house on purpose?"

Then, directly looking at Maddie, he warned, "Ms. Kirkpatrick you need to be vigilant and always watch out for yourself. Here are a couple of my cards with emergency numbers. Keep one with you at all times and place another in a convenient place in your home."

"But Sheriff I know the medical examiner is keeping the skeleton, but can I claim the wardrobe trunk or at least come to your office to check it out. I was so shocked when we saw the skeleton that I didn't get a close look at the trunk. I also know that wardrobe trunks are antiques and considering the shape they are in they could be valuable. So, since it was on my property, don't I own it?"

Yes, Ms. Kirkpatrick, you can come down and take photos of it both inside and out, but we can't release it to you until the investigation is over. Once that is done, it is yours. And after you inspect it, if you find any clues or have ideas of where to look for them, please let me know."

Chapter 20

Maddie phoned the Sheriff determined to make an appointment in order to check out the wardrobe trunk. He assured her the trunk was inside one of their climate controlled storage units. The skeleton was in another storage area. She was glad she didn't have to face the skeleton again. So, when she arrived the Sheriff escorted her to the storage and told her she could stay as long as she wanted.

What Maddie saw was not the trunk she remembered. She must have been so freaked out that day she didn't remember the details. Although old, the trunk was a beautiful forest green with gold grommet detailing and brass hardware. Once polished, it would gleam. The wardrobe trunk reminded her of the stories her aunts and uncles told of the days in the 1920's when they used these wardrobe trunks to carry their clothes and other possessions when they travelled to summer camp and to college. The wardrobe trunks were their mobile closets.

"Why don't they use them today?" Maddie wondered.

She clicked some photos of the outside. The Sheriff had left the trunk unlocked so she photographed all the intricate details of the inside—the rod with its hangers, the many drawers on one side resembling a chest of drawers for one's underwear, scarves, blouses and sweaters. Then, below there were built in pockets for shoes and above that were clips for hanging necklaces and bracelets, and finally, a velvet pad with slits for rings.

Maddie thought she could use the wardrobe trunk as a closet in one of the small lighthouse bedrooms. To travel today with something like this would be impossible. Back in the days of the 1920's, 30's, 40's, and even 50's and 60's, when her relatives traveled they always had porters to help them. She would have to look into other wardrobe trunks to use as closets for all the bedrooms in the lighthouse but first she'd check with Bob Wilkins to see if they would fit into the bedrooms he was designing.

As she closed the door to the trunk, she inspected the underside once again. Running her hand over the decorative grommets, she noticed one was missing. Most grommets would be impossible to remove or even fall off during a rough trip. She would have to find someone who was an expert in finding and securing grommets to any type of trunk. Just another thing she would have to add to her 'to do' list.

= = = = = **CHAPTER 21** = = = =

Maddie was amazed at how fast progress was being made on both houses. Brad had added two more men so work could simultaneously continue on the keeper's house and the lighthouse. The weather had also been very kind to them.

As she left her hotel in Munising, a thought came to Maddie that she would love to treat her workers every once in a while to show her appreciation. She went directly to the lighthouse to find Brad. The workers pointed her to the Gallery Deck. Getting to the Gallery Deck was a work out requiring her to walk up a steep spiral staircase. She would be glad when the elevator was finished.

"Hey, Maddie, you must be out of breath after that climb. What can I do for you."

"It's not that, but what I'd like to do for you and your men. I would like to treat them to a lunch of Pasties today."

"Wow, that would be great."

"Okay, Brad, I'll go around this morning to get their order, then will phone it in. I'll also remember to ask for their initials since that is the Pasty tradition. Then, they will be delivered to the lighthouse. I will also include a drink order."

Taking out her notebook, Maddie started with the workers on the Gallery Deck, then slowly descended the spiral staircase, stopping along the way as she passed other workers. The last couple of orders came from the keeper's house. Maddie added her order to the list. All the orders were different including several combinations of meats, cheeses, vegetables and most with the traditional base of potato and onion. She even stopped at

Glenn's house since he had been so helpful and welcoming to her. He gladly added his order.

Maddie drove to town and found the 'Upper Peninsula's Famous Pasty Restaurant where she had dined. The older gentleman who had waited on her the first night she was in town took her order and promised he would make them in the traditional way with each Pasty individually wrapped with the customer's name, and, of course, the customer's initials pressed into the crust.

"My delivery boy, Johnny, will deliver them to the lighthouse and I'll call you when he is on the his way. So, he will be delivering all the Pasties and the drinks."

Maddie thanked him and drove back to Glenn's house to wait for the order.

"Johnny, the Pasties orders for the workmen out at the lighthouse are finished. I am calling Ms. Kirkpatrick to tell her you are on your way. She will be waiting at the front door to the lighthouse."

The delivery boy picked up the three big bags then returned for the drinks. As he got back to his car, the driver of the car parked next to him yelled, "Hey kid, do you want to make fifty bucks. I'm sure you have a lot to do or maybe want a break, so I can deliver these for you. Where is the delivery going?"

"Out to the Shipwreck Coast. There's a lighthouse under construction and these are for the workers. I should check with my boss first."

"I'm going in that direction anyway. How about if I pay you $ 75. That's a great rate for such a short drive."

Hesitating as he fought the temptation, Johnny finally gave in and handed the man the food and drinks.

"Here's your $ 75. Kid. Don't worry I'll get them there as fast as I can. Now, you go and treat yourself to a good lunch or outing."

Once the car was out of sight, the driver pulled over onto the shoulder of the road. After a few minutes he continued on his way.

In her very efficient way, Maddie was standing in front of the lighthouse to greet the lunch. As the old brown car pulled up, the man asked if she were Ms. Kirkpatrick.

"Yes I am, and are you Johnny?"

"No, Madame, I'm standing in for him today."

Maddie with the help of Brad retrieved the lunches and drinks and paid the driver a tip. Brad offered to distribute the lunches and drinks to the men. So, Maddie took Glenn's lunch to him.

"Come on in Maddie. I see you have our lunches. Please stay and join me in your Pasty treat."

Settling next to Glenn's roaring fireplace with its tall flames, they opened their lunches so see some of the biggest and most delicious Pasties Glenn had ever seen.

"How about a little wine to celebrate?"

"Well, somewhere in the world it is five o'clock, Glenn, so I would love some."

There was very little conversation as they munched their Pasties. Maddie was a vegetarian so her Pasty was filled with an assortment of vegetables with the potato and onion base. Glenn had chosen chicken and vegetables with the same traditional base.

Feeling prematurely full, Maddie didn't think she could finish it and decided to eat the rest for dinner. Although her Pasty was delicious, it seemed to have a different taste from the first time she had experienced the delicacy.

"Glenn, I'm tasting a kind of metallic taste in mine. How about yours?"

"Mine is delicious and, no, I don't have that metallic taste and I don't remember ever tasting metallic in the many years I've eaten them."

Maddie sipped some more wine, then sat back, and looking into the fire started wondering why she was feeling weird. Without realizing it, she let out a groan as her hand instantly touched her stomach.

"I don't know what's wrong Glenn, but I'm starting to get sharp pains in my stomach." She immediately left to go to the bathroom where nausea quickly joined her symptoms. When she returned to the living room Glenn could see her face had turned a grayish white.

"Can I get you anything, Maddie?"

"Thanks, but not right now. I'm feeling so dizzy and my fingers feel numb, and am getting these horrible headaches. I never get headaches."

As he finished his Pasty, Glenn, who had become very worried, kept his eyes on Maddie as he felt that it was reaching the point where he should call the ambulance. It wasn't until Maddie put her hand over her chest and mumbled, "I've never felt this, but my heart is beating out of control."

"Maddie, I'm calling an ambulance. We can't wait any longer. The hospital in Munising is very good and I will drive behind the ambulance and stay with you."

By the time Glenn heard the ambulance siren, he could tell Maddie was having trouble breathing and was becoming confused.

The ambulance attendant took her vital signs and gently put her on a stretcher, and took her to the ambulance where they immediately strapped an oxygen mask over her face.

The attendant turned to Glenn and asked, "When did the symptoms start?"

He told them about twenty minutes after she had eaten part of her Pasty.

"Do not throw her food away, Mr. Pedersen. We will need to test it."

As the ambulance was leaving, Glenn could see Brad approaching the lodge.

"What's going on Glenn?"

After Glenn explained the situation, Brad told Glenn that none of his men had become sick.

"This seems to be very suspicious, Brad, so I am going to the hospital. Maddie needs to know there is someone in the waiting room for her.

Glenn packed up Maddie's half eaten Pasty and drink and put them in the refrigerator. After taking Toby on a short walk he drove to the hospital in Munising.

Fortunately, the small hospital was not that crowded. Glenn registered at the desk that he was there for Madeline Kirkpatrick who had arrived by ambulance.

"Are you related to Ms Kirkpatrick in any way, Mr. Pedersen?"

Upon hearing that Glenn was a friend, the nurse asked about her family and where they were.

"I don't think Ms. Kirkpatrick has any family in the area. Her parents have died, and I don't think she has any siblings."

"Do you know, Mr. Pedersen, if she has a medical directive or a living will?"

"No, I don't, but I do know she is working with an attorney regarding her properties on the Ship Wreck Coast although I don't know his name. I assume he lives in Sault Ste. Marie, Michigan. Since she is working with an architect and the owner of one of the biggest construction companies in Sault Ste. Marie, I'll bet they have an idea of who he would be. Ms. Kirkpatrick is a very savvy and efficient business woman. If you want, I could call around to the nearby law firms."

"That would be helpful, Mr. Pedersen, just in case we need it, but right now we are still assessing her situation and will let you know when we have more information."

Glenn chose a chair in the corner of the waiting room so he could quietly think through the whole situation. Picking up his smart phone he googled law firms in or near Sault Ste. Marie. The name Hagan, Hagan and Kalburg sounded familiar. He surmised it must be a family run law firm which was typical in that area. Since Glenn knew it would take a while for them to run tests, then get the results, he decided to return to the lighthouse to ask Brad if he had an idea of who her attorney might be. On his way out he stopped at the nurses desk to let them knew that he would be back shortly.

"Mr. Pedersen could you bring back the food Ms. Kirkpatrick was eating before she felt sick. We will then start testing it."

Brad was surprised to see Glenn. "So, how is Maddie?"

Glenn explained that they were still running tests on her and he had come back for her food as the hospital wanted to test it too.

"I also wanted to ask you, Brad, if you knew the name or firm of her lawyer. The hospital wants to know if she has a medical directive. It is just routine and more important since she has no living relatives."

Brad thought for a moment, then went back to his truck for his records and paperwork.

"Okay, Glenn, I'm not sure but my firm uses Hagan, Hagan, and Kalberg. I think Bob Wilkins may use them too. They are very reliable and reputable. There's also one other smaller firm which is very reputable too, and that is Nilsen and Solbery. I would check with both firms, and if they won't give you information since you're not a relative ask the hospital to call. They would probably give the information to them. I also know the larger firm which I use has a branch office in Duluth and since she bought the lighthouse in Duluth at an auction and sometimes the laws are different in another state which may be more flexible in getting information on someone."

Glenn and Brad exchanged phone numbers. Then Glenn returned to the hospital with Maddie's half eaten Pasty and gave it to her nurse.

"Mr. Pedersen, we now have Ms. Kirkpatrick stabilized, and she is resting comfortably but has been sedated. I'll get the doctor so he can tell you more. She'll probably stay in the hospital for a few days. You can go sit in her room. Just go down the hall, turn to the left and she is in room 116."

Glenn quietly entered Maddie's room. Her eyes were closed. He whispered her name. Slowly opening her eyes, she smiled.

"They are going to test your food, Maddie, so I brought your Pasty to the hospital. They should know soon what made you so sick. Is there anyone I can call for you? I didn't think you had any relatives around here, but is there a good friend?"

She whispered, "Please call Erick Dawson. His private phone number is in my purse. He is a very dear friend."

Her purse was on a side table. Glenn looked through the different zippered compartments and pockets then found a little red address book which also listed phone numbers.

"Maddie, I found Erick Dawson's phone numbers in your red phone book. There are two numbers. Should I call the one that says personal number or the one that is labeled shipping company?"

Maddie told him to call the personal number. She then fell asleep and Glenn walked down to the hospital gift shop and florist, purchased a bouquet of spring flowers then returned to her room and placed them on her window sill before quietly leaving.

A doctor was walking towards her room and seeing Glenn asked if he were a relative.

"No, doctor, I am not. She has no relatives nearby. I'm just a good friend."

The doctor assured him she was improving and he thought she had had a reaction to something she had eaten. They would probably know by the next day what had caused her sickness, then continued:

"Just to let you know, I think this was very serious and she was lucky to have such a good friend with her when it happened. I understand from the nurses that you are the one who brought in her leftover food for testing. Thanks for acting so quickly. You probably saved her life."

Glenn knew it was serious, but was stunned when the doctor meant it was life threatening.

Toby met Glenn at his front door.

"Hi boy, do you need to go out? Just for a short time. I have phone calls to make."

Upon returning from their short walk, Glenn poured some dog food in Toby's bowl and refilled his water dish, then sat down at his desk to check the phone numbers for the law firms. He started with Hogan Hogan and Kalburg.

"Hello, this is Glenn Pedersen calling. I am a friend of Madeline Kirkpatrick, who owns the Twin Sisters Inn in Sault Ste Marie, and am trying to find out who her lawyer is since she has become ill and the hospital wants to know if she has a medical directive or a living will. Is she your client?"

The receptionist answered:

"We don't give out private information on our clients, but I can tell you if she has an account here."

After a few minutes checking information on her computer, she answered, "Yes, she is on our client list but only she can release this information. If it is imminent, and she can't speak for herself, please have the hospital call us."

Thanking the receptionist, Glenn immediately called the hospital to relay the information. If Maddie were awake the next day, she could certainly call the law firm to send to the hospital whatever information they needed.

Glenn dialed the number for Maddie's friend, Erick Dawson and got through to him immediately. Erick thanked him and said he was in port, and would come immediately.

■ = ■ = ■ = ■ **CHAPTER 22** ■ = ■ = ■ =

Maddie was just finishing breakfast when there was a soft knock at her door. Before she could answer, she heard a click, then saw a beautiful bouquet of spring flowers appear around the corner of the wall that led to the door.

"How beautiful", she remarked which was immediately followed by the identity of the one holding the bouquet.

"For a beautiful lady on a beautiful sunny morning."

A smiling Erick Dawson walked over and kissed Maddie on the forehead.

"Oh Erick, I'm so glad you're here. Now, I really feel safe."

"Well, my love, I couldn't stay away. I had to see how the sweetest lady I've every known was pulling through a tough situation. So, what landed you in this situation?"

"Erick, I don't know. The last I remember was eating lunch, than feeling ill and sort of blanking out and finally realizing I was in the hospital."

She continued the story about how she had treated the construction guys to a lunch of Pasties and how she remembered helping to hand them out, then eating half of hers at Glenn's lodge before feeling ill.

"It sounds, Maddie, as though the first thing we'll have to do is check the shop where you bought the Pasties."

"But Erick, it has been in the town for years and has a wonderful reputation. I ate Pasties there the first night I was here and everything was fine. The construction workers ate them also and nobody got sick."

A knock on the door interrupted their conversation. A doctor entered the room.

"Ms. Kirkpatrick we have the results of your tests. The lab tested the uneatened part of the Pasty, and there were traces of arsenic laced through out the crust and food. Your symptoms are those of arsenic poisoning. Did anyone else in your group get sick?"

"Not that I know of doctor."

"So, Ms. Kirkpatrick, we have already reported this to the police and they are treating it as an attempted murder. They are sending over two police officers to guard your door."

Erick stepped forward and introduced himself as a long time friend, then assured the doctor he would be watching out for her.

"Ms. Kirkpatrick, we would like to keep you here for two more nights of observation."

"Maddie, when the two police officers arrive, I'm going to talk to the manager of the Pasty store to see if I can pick up any clues. I would also like to meet Glenn who phoned me, then check on the construction and meet the crew. I'll report back to you as soon as possible."

"Erick, you need to talk to Brad who is head of the construction. He is very honest and will be of help to you. So is Glenn who has proven to be a wonderful friend. He saved my life."

CHAPTER 23

Erick had no problem finding the Upper Peninsula's Famous Pasty Shop. As he entered the shop and restaurant combination, the manager/owner Mr. Olson, was busy ordering supplies. Fortunately, there were no customers since it was after lunchtime. He invited Erick to sit down. Erick immediately launched into the story.

The manager mentioned that the police had already called to alert him that they would be visiting his shop. The frustrated manager also added that he would probably be visited by the health department and that there would be an extensive investigation.

"Mr. Dawson, I can assure you that we've never had an incident in our thirty year history. Unless Ms. Kirkpatrick had an allergy to one of the ingredients, I can't imagine what happened."

"Mr. Olson, we were just informed by the hospital lab that arsenic had been laced throughout her Pasty, but obviously none of the others."

"Wow, someone must have had it in for her, but how did they get inside the Pasty. I checked all the Pasties as they were made and saw nothing of the kind."

"Mr. Olson, who delivered the Pasties to the construction site?"

"It was Johnny, our delivery boy. He's in the back working on some extra chores. I'll go get him and bring him up front so we can talk to him."

As Mr. Olson disappeared through the doors to the back room, Erick took the chance to look around the restaurant and shop. He noticed that everything was very clean and stored very neatly on the shelves. Mr. Olson seemed to run a very clean operation.

When Mr. Olson returned with a nervous Johnny, they briefed the delivery boy on what had transpired. Mr. Olson probed:

"Johnny, did you notice anything different about the delivery to the construction site?"

Johnny hung his head and made no eye contact with Mr. Olson or Erick.

"Johnny, what's wrong son? I'd rather you be honest with us. I also know you're very honest. How was the delivery different from the others? The police are going to want to know."

Trying to hold back tears, Johnny spoke in a low voice.

"I took the food to my car and just as I put in the last packages, a man who was parked next to me asked if I wanted to make some money. He said he was going in the direction of the Ship Wreck Coast anyway and offered me seventy five dollars. I figured he was from around here or at least looked like it so I gave him the Pasties and drinks and he gave me the money."

"Thank you for being so honest, Johnny. Ms. Kirkpatrick knows Johnny so hopefully the police can get a description from her. And Johnny, at the end of the business day, we're going to sit and have a big talk about security. You should have known better or at least let me know so I could have checked this guy out."

Erick felt for Johnny, but kids had to learn some tough lessons. The question would be how to trace this guy and perhaps the lab could tell how the poison got into the Pasty.

As Erick approached the hospital, he wondered how much Maddie would remember about the delivery person. Knocking on her door before entering, an alert Maddie looked up.

"Erick, did you learn anything new?"

Sitting down by her bed, Erick took her hand in his and replied, "Yes, I've learned a lot so far but not enough. I visited the Pasty shop and talked to Mr. Olson, the owner. We both learned that Johnny, the delivery boy, didn't deliver the Pasties to the construction site. A man approached him outside the store and offered him seventy five dollars if Johnny would let him deliver the Pasties. So, I was wondering if you could describe the man."

"I do know Johnny. Brad and I was surprised when the other guy delivered the Pasties, but I thought he was a new employee as he said he was standing in for Johnny that day. He had an old brown car. Brad, our construction manager, helped me hand the Pasties and drinks out to the men so you should also talk to Brad."

"So, Maddie, do you remember what he looked like. The police will want to know."

"Well, he was about 5'9" tall which is short for a man. At least I think so. He seemed kind of scruffy. He was going bald at the front of his head so his hair was receding. His hair color was dark brown. He wore a dirty jacket and very worn jeans. But, he seemed nice enough."

"Maddie, If you are feeling okay, I'll go talk to Brad to see if he can shed more light on this."

Erick bent down and kissed Maddie on the check.

"I think when you're released from the hospital, you should go back to The Twin Sisters Inn to rest for a few days."

"Erick, I have an extra room and would love for you to stay at the inn as long as you want."

"Now, who could resist that? I'd love to. See you later. Am going to talk to Brad. Hope he can take a break at the construction site."

On his way to the construction site, Erick stopped at the Pasty shop to buy a Pasty. He had never had one before. Since it was late afternoon, it was the perfect time. He could eat it on the way to to the site.

Chapter 24

When Erick arrived at the construction site, it was late afternoon and although daylight savings time had begun a few weeks before, it still became dark early.

The men were still hard at work. As he approached the lighthouse, he asked the men if he could speak to Brad. As Erick was marveling at the scenery, Brad came around from the lake front of the lighthouse.

"Brad, I'm Erick Dawson, a close friend of Maddie Kirkpatrick. I've just visited her in the hospital and she's doing fine. Did you know that the delivery boy from the Pasty shop was not the regular one, and wanted to know if you could give us a description of the man who actually delivered the Pasties."

Brad thought for a moment then described the man very much the same as Maddie's description.

"The one thing that I remember which Maddie might not have known was that as he handed over the lunches he seemed very impatient and acted as though he wanted to get out of here as fast as possible. Also, even though our weather is still quite cool, I noticed drops of perspiration on his forehead. Perhaps he was just nervous but if he were an honest guy there would be no reason for nervousness. After all, my crew is very friendly and appreciative. So, when do you think Maddie will be back?"

Erick explained that she probably would be released the next day and go back to her inn in Sault St. Marie for a while to rest.

"Don't worry Brad, I'll keep an eye on her. She'll be safe with me hanging around."

"Tell her Erick, that I will come and see her in a few days since we have to talk about paint colors for the lighthouse and keeper's house. Give her my best. Thanks so much and it was great to meet you."

Erick decided to introduce himself to Glenn before returning to the hospital. He was greeted at the front door by Toby and Glenn. After introductions, Glenn invited him in for a drink and as they sat in front of the fireplace, Erick told Glenn what he knew and Glenn shared his story from the beginning before the construction when he would see a flashlight moving through the lighthouse and keeper's house. He also shared how he was knocked out one rainy night as he was walking toward the lighthouse to check out the source of the lights. And, of course, there was the story of finding the trunk and skeleton in the basement of the keeper's house.

"So, you see Erick, weird things were going on in those buildings well before Maddie bought the lighthouse. There must be something in there that someone is desperate to find enough to engage in the attempted murder of Maddie. We really need to search the lighthouse and keeper's house thoroughly and to let Brad and his crew know that if they find anything, they should tell us immediately."

The morning of Maddie's release from the hospital, Erick suggested he drive her to The Twin Sisters Inn.

"On our way to the inn, Maddie, we'll stop by the construction site to see if one of the guys would be willing to drive your car to the inn."

When they arrived at the lighthouse, Erick suggested Maddie stay in the car. It was a very chilly day for Spring. Erick found Brad in the keeper's house where they devised a plan for the cars. Brad suggested that he would drive Maddie's car to the inn, then stay in town for the day so he and Maddie could choose paint colors for the houses. Then one of her staff could drive Brad back to the site with enough time to return to Sault Ste. Marie in the evening.

When Erick told Maddie the plan, she felt good that her staff would share in the car transfer. As Erick pulled into the parking for The Twin Sisters Inn, he remarked, "Although I've guided my freighters through the Soo Locks many times, I am looking forward to seeing your town from a tourist's point of view and to get really get to know the town."

Chapter 25

The next morning seemed to appear out of nowhere. Both Maddie and Erick had overslept. Matt and Heidi were manning the front desk even though the guest traffic was low.

After breakfast, Brad sat down with Maddie to talk about which colors to use on the lighthouse. Erick was invited to participate in the discussion. The lighthouse needed a new paint job so Brad described which colors would work the best.

"Since the lighthouse is on a cliff over looking Lake Superior with the background being a forest, I would suggest using a white paint since it is against a darker background. You would then have to choose what is called the 'daymark.' Lighthouse towers are given special painted patterns such as diamond shapes, or spirals or stripes, etc in a color that would distinguish the lighthouse tower from other lighthouses nearby. The common colors for these daymarks are red or black."

Maddie thought for a minute, then answered, "I definitely like the white, and think I would choose red spirals wrapped around the lighthouse."

Brad agreed then asked what color she wanted for the keeper's house so that it would be a good match.

"I think I will choose white with a red trim. And I also plan on putting a white picket fence around the yard that faces the lake and cliff especially for families with kids to keep them from playing too close to the cliff. I also hope to have a screened in porch or deck on the lake side of the house so guests can sit and relax with the sound of the waves and also watch the freighters sail by. We could have afternoon happy hours on the porch or deck."

"So, you want the one picket fence to be large enough to enclose the lake side of the lighthouse and keeper's house. That way you would have a very large yard for children to play safely."

Maddie confirmed that and added, "I know some people like to go to the top of the cliff and look over, but for me, that is too much of a liability. If they want to do that they'll have to go off my property. The fence should mark the property line in back of each structure and to the sides of the buildings."

Erick then chimed in, "What about the front yard. You could extend the fence along the sides to the buildings then along the sides to your front yard that faces Glenn's house then enclose in your front property line. Tourists would have to come in through your front yard gate and there would still be a large expanse of lawn between your front yard and Glenn's backyard."

Brad laughed. "So, you want your guests fenced in."

Maddie smiled and replied that she was concerned about the safety of the guests and their children, and the liability that she would have being so close to the cliff, then added one more thing.

"Brad, since the breakfast room and lounge will be in the keeper's house, how about building an enclosed glass walkway which would be temperature controlled, so the lighthouse guests wouldn't have to worry about going outside just to get breakfast. I can't imagine tourists will be here in the winter, but the hunters will stay here then. The weather can be brutal at that time of year. But even in the spring, summer and fall the weather can be cold and rainy."

Both Brad and Erick agreed. Brad said the next time they had a meeting, he would tell her about the light in the lighthouse and arrange for her to meet someone from the Coast Guard since they are the inspectors of the light."

At the front desk, Maddie asked Matt if he would drive Brad back to the construction site. Heidi could man the desk and Maddie would help if needed. Erick volunteered to ride with Matt so he wouldn't have to return alone.

After they had left the inn, Maddie went over to see if Heidi needed help at the front desk. She could see that Heidi wasn't that happy about it. She wondered why Heidi seemed so inflexible at times. She didn't know anyone in town and she lived at the inn which was so convenient, and fit within her budget. It was almost as if she had a secret. If Heidi were more than a student or had some kind of agenda, Maddie was determined to find out.

Maddie felt there was a degree of danger around her based on what had happened to her within the last few weeks with her being poisoned and hospitalized. She trusted Erick, Glenn and Brad. Brad had thoroughly vetted his construction crew, but Heidi was the mysterious one. After all, Maddie had just met her on the plane to Sault Ste. Marie. Perhaps she had made a mistake befriending her so quickly. She really didn't know that much about her background. Maddie felt an urgent need to check her out again. Perhaps, Erick would have some ideas. Going back into her memory, she realized that all the strange happenings at the lighthouse and then the poisoned Pasty all had happened after Heidi came to town.

Maddie decided to retire to her bedroom and told Heidi she could close up at 9 PM since business was slow. Matt had a key so he and Erick would have no problem getting in. She was determined to talk to Erick the next morning to formulate a plan so they could run a thorough check on Heidi without her knowledge.

CHAPTER 26

As Maddie awoke the next morning, the sun was streaming through her windows.

"Everything is new and fresh in the morning," She thought.

A new feeling of positivity engulfed her and she felt as if there were a path to the truth.

Erick was already in the breakfast room. As Maddie passed the front desk, Heidi called out to her.

"Maddie, Erick left his keys here last night before he left with Matt. Could you give them to him if you're going to breakfast?"

Maddie thanked her and went to join Erick.

"Wow, I never realized the keys were missing since Matt had his. There are some important keys on that ring too like the lighthouse and keeper's house keys, and to certain places on the freighter."

"Erick, I didn't know you already had keys to the lighthouse and also the keeper's house."

"Brad thought I should have them and Maddie, this brings me to something I wanted to share with you. Before I had ever heard of your accident, I had been seriously considering retiring from the freighter business because I need a more stable life. I was planning on coming out to see you anyway, and more importantly to be with you. You are very special to me, Maddie. So, I would love to help you with the construction or anything you need to get your project finished. and, as much as I love staying in your inn, I want to pay my own way, so I'll pay for my room and when the keeper's house is available, will stay there. In addition to Glenn you will have two people watching over your property. I want to protect you, Maddie, and I won't let anything else happen to you."

Maddie was stunned. Tears welled up in her eyes as she felt the same about Erick.

"Erick, you don't know how I would love for you to be here."

She reached across the table to touch his hand, then told him her thoughts about Heidi.

She spoke in a low voice hoping no one would hear her.

"I have some ideas about how we can handle this."

"Fine, let's go out to lunch. I would love to sample your fine restaurants in Sault St. Marie."

"Do you like seafood, Erick?"

"I sure do."

"There are many fine restaurants here including the dining room in our main hotel, The Ojibway Inn which has huge beautiful windows looking out onto the park which one has to walk through to see the freighters going through the locks. That's a special park as it is controlled by Homeland Security for the safety of the freighters coming from all over the world which have to pass through those locks."

Maddie also thought of another popular restaurant since they both liked seafood. It was the Lock View restaurant located across from the entrance to the Soo locks. Erick chose the Lock View since it sounded better for lunchtime. They decided to meet in the lobby of the inn at 12:30pm.

"And one more thing, Maddie, until we meet for lunch I have some contacts who may be able to find out something about Heidi so I need to phone them."

Maddie was amenable and asked Erick if he could go back to her office where she could show him Heidi's personnel sheet with the information she had given her.

"As you can see, Erick, there is nothing that stands out here. She grew up in Holland, and her parents are still living there and are near retirement. She is twenty and has had a few small jobs, but like many young women who come to the United States, they simply want to have a travel adventure, but mainly want to improve their speaking ability of the English language."

"Maddie, do you have any idea where she goes on her lunch hour?"

"No," Maddie replied. "But, maybe we could start there. She doesn't have a car or drivers license for ID, only a passport. Wherever she goes she would have to walk or take a bus."

"Are you saying we should follow her?" Erick replied.

"Yes, I am and we should do it right away. I guess you and I could take turns, so do you want me to start or would you like to."

"I don't want you to be in danger, Maddie, so I'll start today to see what degree of danger there is. With that in mind, let's push our lunch back to an early dinner today."

Maddie checked at the front desk to see what Matt and Heidi's lunch schedules were.

"Matt, I am letting Heidi go first today since she worked late last night. She will be leaving at noon and please tell her that she can take an extra half hour today and then you can too since I will be here all day. So, Matt, I'm doing this since both of you have carried a full load the last few days and have worked very hard."

Erick was in his room talking on the phone to his contacts when Maddie knocked on the door to alert him to the change in Matt's and Heidi's lunchtime schedules.

"Fine, I'll be ready at noon to follow Heidi. Will be back around 3:30 or 4pm then we can go out to an early dinner. See you then, but I have to get back to my calls now."

CHAPTER 27

A few minutes before noon, Erick entered the lobby to look at the brochure rack of tours by the front door. He saw Heidi talk to Matt, then take her purse and leave for lunch. As soon as she had cleared the door, he left and watched as she crossed the street to stand at the bus stop. Erick immediately crossed the street and went to his car parked a half a block from the bus stop. He had just gotten in when he saw the bus approaching. It stopped at the bus stop and Heidi stepped on, paid her fare and sat on the right side by the window.

As the bus continued on its way, Erick pulled out into the street and followed. He wasn't sure if Heidi would remember what his car looked like or if she had ever seen it. The bus approached the International Bridge which crossed the St. Mary's River to connect Sault Ste Marie, Michigan, USA to Sault Ste Marie, Ontario, Canada. Erick was glad he remembered to bring his passport, but usually carried it because of his job on the freighters. He knew that Heidi had a passport.

Erick wondered what would take her across the bridge with only an hour and a half for lunch.

He followed the bus onto the bridge and crossed the two and a half mile span where there was a line of cars waiting to go through customs. He reached for his passport.

As the bus passed through customs, the driver showed his passport then pulled over to a parking space where a customs agent boarded the bus to check the passports of the passengers.

After Erick passed through customs, he drove over to park a few spaces down from the bus.. Just outside the parking lot, Erick spied the Ontario Visitors Center. The bus also went to the visitors center where the passengers would disembark. He saw the passengers leave the bus to walk to their destinations. Heidi didn't appear. She was still on the bus. Once the bus backed out of the parking lot, it did go a couple tenths of a mile to the visitor center. Erick followed and parked his car across from the center. With his eyes glued to the bus door, he finally saw Heidi leave the bus. She walked over to the center where there was a brochure stand. Erick was wondering if the brochure stand was a meeting place for someone. Sure enough, within a few minutes a black car moved to the stand. Erick could see a man was at the wheel, but he wasn't close enough to identify him. Heidi went over to the man and said something to him then walked around to the passenger's side of the car, opened the door and got in. The car began to drive off through the city. Erick followed, but from a distance. After a couple of turns, the driver of the car found a parking spot in front of an Italian restaurant. Erick got a better look at the man. He was of medium height with black hair. The couple entered the restaurant.

The restaurant had big windows with lace curtains which were pulled back. Fortunately, for Erick, the couple's table was in front of the window so Erick could see them clearly. Erick had his smart phone so decided to take their picture to show Maddie. He then moved his car past the restaurant for about a half a block then got out and crossed the street and walked back towards the restaurant. He took a picture of the building, but had to get closer to take a good picture of the couple.

Erick had a hood on his jacket and pulled it over his head. There was a bus stop to the side of the window. Erick stood on the curb by the bus stop so he could be sure he could get a decent picture of the couple. Their food and drinks had just been served to them. He first took their pictures separately. One picture of the man and one of Heidi. Then contorting himself in such a way that he couldn't be seen, he took two pictures as close as he could get to them showing both of them eating and drinking. Then he saw them exchanging white envelopes. He took a picture of that. It made it look like a business lunch. But, who would she be in business with?

As surprising as this was to Erick, he knew that whatever happened or was going to happen, his pictures probably would not hold up in court. Erick looked at his watch. Heidi only had about forty minutes to get back. How would she do it having to wait for busses and going through customs on the United States side of the bridge.

Within ten minutes or so, Heidi and the man left the restaurant for the man's car. The car then made a U-turn and headed back to the International Bridge. Erick ran across the street and followed in his car. Even though it was lunch time, the bridge wasn't crowded and Heidi wasn't in a bus, but stayed in her friend's car thus saving time. Going through customs was easy, then it was only a few minutes to the Twin Sisters Inn. The man's car passed the inn so she would not be seen. Heidi left the man's car and walked a half a block to the inn. Erick had not seen anything suggesting a romantic relationship. There was no hugging before leaving the car, so Erick assumed it was business.

Once Heidi had entered the inn, Erick drove past the inn and parked a block away then walked back to the inn, went around to the back and entered through the back door then took the back elevator so he wouldn't be seen. He couldn't wait to tell Maddie about his stake out.

CHAPTER 28

Maddie and Erick met at the front desk, then decided to walk to the Lock View Restaurant which was just a few blocks from the inn. Almost everything in the small town of Sault Ste. Marie was within walking distance.

The Lock View Restaurant was located across from the entrance to the Soo Locks. The restaurant's slogan was, "The fish you eat today slept last night in Whitefish Bay."

Perusing the menu, Maddie pointed out to Erick that the variety of fish they prepared were local to the area.

"Look, Erick, the two main fish dishes 'White fish and Walleye' which are the Great Lakes specialties are prepared in so many ways."

Erick saw pan fried, broiled and lemon peppered plus cajun, and deep fried. Maddie also suggested that the crab legs were excellent and so was the homemade coleslaw. And, as always, one could get the traditional Pasty. She shuddered after she said that due to her recent experience, but knew that Pasties were the rage of the Upper Peninsula. She eventually knew she would have the courage again to eat the meat and cheese Pasties.

"Erick, in some restaurants here there is even 'construction cheese dip.' I'm sure Brad knows about that, but whatever they have in this town, it's delicious."

Maddie ordered the Walleye and Erick ordered the Whitefish. The vegetable sides were tasty and all went perfectly with the regional wine they ordered. To top off the night, they ordered dessert and Irish coffee. As they were enjoying the Irish coffee, their conversation turned to what Erick saw as he followed Heidi.

Now, Maddie, when I tell you this, it's just what I witnessed, and I don't know who the guy was she met or if anything illegal is going on. It was just so strange since she never acknowledged that she knew anyone around here. So, here is what I saw."

Maddie listened and became concerned but felt they needed more.

"Erick, the sheriff told us that with all these events which have happened, there has to be something they or someone is searching for which is linked to my property on the Shipwreck Coast."

Erick showed Maddie the pictures he had taken of the couple in the restaurant.

"What do you think of these? Who is Heidi's secret friend? Also, Maddie we need to thoroughly inspect your properties, the keeper's house and the lighthouse, and I mean every nook and cranny. Maybe there's something outside in the yard that could give us a clue."

"I agree Erick, so we need to start immediately. But how do we do this safely?"

"My only thought, Maddie, is that I'm going to join the construction crew so I can be on the property everyday in both the lighthouse and keeper's house. I will just tell Brad that I will help with anything he needs. I'd even be happy cleaning up the place so I can search around."

"What if Brad can't pay you", Maddie asked.

"Then, I'll just say I'm doing this just for you. Remember, I have my back pay, then my retirement will pop in."

Maddie suggested that she would call Brad in the morning to inform him of Erick's offer to help in any way.

"But, Erick, I want you to stay here at the inn until a room in the keeper's house can be fixed up for you. I can have a bed, chest of drawers and lamps moved out there. I want you to be comfortable. Oh, and also, while staying at the inn, would you please keep an eye on Heidi?"

Then on second thought, she added, "Once you are staying on the property in the keeper's house, I will be out there most days to check on the remodeling progress and will also check around the buildings for any clues which can tell us what happened."

Erick squeezed her hand. "What would I do without you."

As they walked arm in arm down the street towards the inn, the town was calm and peaceful. Approaching the inn, they could see that

Heidi and Matt had locked up and closed for the night with everything in its place.

They could not have known that in an old house across the street on the second floor was a telescope and camera pointed at the front of the inn watching the coming and goings of its residents.

CHAPTER 29

By the time Maddie had finished breakfast then checked on the front desk, Erick had already left for the construction site. She decided to leave early in order to begin checking around the construction site and grounds, then a thorough search of the two buildings. She was determined to find a clue. Then, perhaps Brad could also talk to her about the condition of the light and fog alarm at the lighthouse.

One last survey of the inn told her all was normal. The maids were busy changing sheets and vacuuming the rooms and hallway. Matt and Heidi had reservations under control.

Stopping at the front desk, Maddie informed Matt that he would be in charge for the day since she wouldn't be back until evening. "If you need me just call on the cell phone. I'll be easy to reach."

The sunny clear day put her in an optimistic mood as she drove along the country roads to the Shipwreck Coast. Parking in the semi finished lot in front of the keeper's house she walked back across the lawn to Glenn's house. He had seen her drive in so was at his front door.

"How are you feeling? Toby and I are about to go for a walk. Would you like to accompany us?"

"Thanks, Glenn, just thought I would let you know I'm here in case you need anything. I'm starting a thorough check of the grounds and both the lighthouse and keeper's house to try to find any clues which might tell me why these strange and dangerous things may be happening.

"Well, stay safe Maddie, I'll see you later."

Maddie retrieved her work gloves from the car with a few tools and a small rake. She decided to look around the outside of the keeper's house. Since it was quite old and there had been little care of the yard, vines and flowering shrubs were out of control. She pushed aside weeds and raked away some dead flowers. She noticed a retaining wall. A mass of flowering vines had hidden it. She planned on pruning the flowering vine later. Maddie also saw the ground level cellar windows of the house's foundation. Weeds had grown over them also. The windows were so dirty that a hardened crust had formed over them. As she looked around she saw the old breezeway that connected the house to the lighthouse. It was old and open to the outside with only an old roof over the structure, so Maddie was glad she had mentioned to Brad that she wanted a new totally enclosed breezeway which would be temperature regulated so guests wouldn't have to wear their coats in cold weather just to walk to the keeper's house for breakfast. She would have fun decorating the inside of the breezeway with plants and flowers along the enclosed walk which would bloom all year. She might even put the little Italian Christmas lights on it for the holidays.

The front of the keeper's house faced the lawn between it and Glenn's house. The bedrooms in the front would not have a lake view, but of a beautiful green lawn shaded by large old trees. She couldn't wait to see the symphony of fall colors displayed by the sugar maples, and Autumn Blaze Maples among others with their red, yellow, scarlet and burnt orange stunning colors. Finally, finishing with the yard, Maddie entered the keeper's house by the front door. She was in the foyer and to the left was the living room, so she began there. The room extended from the front of the house to the rear. There was a fireplace on the outside wall. An antique looking mantel was over the fireplace. Part of this room would also be the breakfast room.

The rest of the room would serve as lounge. As she walked to the other end of the room she figured that end used to be the dining room since the kitchen was located off that end of the room, thus the reason for making it the breakfast end of the room. She could see that all appliances in the kitchen would have to be replaced by commercial grade appliances.

Returning from the kitchen, she walked down the hall to the foyer. On her left was a front room which probably had been a den. This room would become the keeper's bedroom. A private bath would be installed. Its larger size would allow for a sitting area or small private living room for the keeper.

Upstairs were five bedrooms with two bathrooms on the hall. Looking at the bedrooms reminded her to ask Brad how many bedrooms would fit in the lighthouse.

There was a knock at the door.

"Hi Glenn, have you and Toby finished your walk?"

"I noticed you were scrutinizing the old house, Maddie, and wondered if you needed help."

"How's your botanical knowledge, Glenn?"

"Well, I think I'm pretty good at what's natural around here. What do you want to know?"

Maddie led him to the back of the house to show him the flowered vine cascading over the retaining wall.

"This one is easy, Maddie. This flowering vine is native to this area and is called a 'Blushing Susie Black-eyed Susan Vine.'"

"Glenn, I love the colors and fullness of the vine although it needs some pruning. The pink, yellow, white and orange flowers form a beautiful blanket over the retaining wall."

As Maddie and Glenn studied the vine, Toby began to sniff around the ground and vine. He plunged his nose through the mass of flowers and immediately became excitable as if he were after something.

"What did you find, Toby?" Toby could only whine and become more agitated.

"We better put on our gloves, Maddie, so we can see what Toby is after."

Both started pulling the tangled vines apart. They were stronger than they seemed. Maddie hoped they wouldn't ruin the many flowers.

At last they cleared a hole and saw the gray cement of the retaining wall.

"Be careful, Toby, don't hurt your snout."

As they were able to clear more vines, eventually, there was enough room to touch the wall. They ran their hands over it. Glenn felt a crack and as he followed the crack around, he felt a small hidden latch.

"I think there is more to this wall than we know, Maddie. I'll go back to my house and get some pruning shears. Toby, you stay here with Ms. Kirkpatrick."

Deep in thought about what they would find, Maddie didn't hear or see Erick walking across the lawn.

"Hey, Maddie, I'm taking a short break. What's going on? Can I help?"

"Glenn and I are pruning this beautiful vine and we think we have found something like maybe a small door in the retaining wall. Glenn's coming back with his pruning shears."

"Sounds serious, my dear. Are you sure these vines aren't poisonous?"

"I'm not sure but Glenn said they are native to this area and didn't mention that. If they are he would have known that and warned me."

Toby acted as if he were on steroids as in true Golden Retriever fashion. He was excitedly sniffing everything and at the same time looking back at Maddie and Glenn, who had rejoined the group.

Glenn's pruning only took a few minutes and revealed a small door which was camouflaged into the cement of the wall. One had to look hard to see that it was really there. Glenn tried the small latch which was latched. Glenn looked around then remembered something.

"This is about the same place where I was hit over the head that rainy night before I ever met you, Maddie, and before the lighthouse was auctioned off. I wonder if I can find a key in the keeper's house or lighthouse and if not, we'll have to jimmy the lock."

Feeling as though he were on the fringe of the conversation, Erick chimed in "I don't think we should waste anytime looking for a key. Anyone can tell that these vines have been messed with so it will reveal that this could be a place for something valuable. If we can break the lock, whatever we find, we won't return it to this place, but keep it safe somewhere else."

Glenn went to retrieve his tool box.

"Maddie this could be serious and since you mean so much to me, I don't want you in any danger. Only you, I and Glenn know about this. Toby does too and I think his excitement might be some kind of dog recollection of the night Glenn was attacked. No matter what we find, we can't tell anyone on the site, not even Brad. As much as I trust him, it is easy to have a slip of the tongue and news travels fast. If someone is watching us and this site, who knows what they'll do."

Fortunately, Glenn returned with the right tools to break the lock open. The door opened to reveal a shaft rather than a vault. Glenn had a commercial grade flashlight, and lying down on his stomach was able to inch over to the opening and shine it straight down. He yelled back, "It looks to be about twenty feet deep. This opening is enough for one man to crawl through and there are rock steps built into the dirt. If one of us goes down he should have a rope tied around him so we can steady him from above. I don't know how we're going to do this without causing a commotion."

Erick stepped forward and volunteered to go down into the shaft.

"I have some rescue equipment in my car which is from the freighter. When there are violent storms, high winds, and huge waves on the lakes, the men still have to go on deck to check hatch covers and other things. So, they are buckled to ropes which create a path for them to do their inspections without being thrown overboard to a certain death. I know how to rig this up so I'm sure I can get down the shaft and retrieve whatever." Maddie was immediately frightened.

"Erick, I don't want you to risk your life just for my project."

"I'll do anything for the woman I love."

Maddie silently gasped. That was the first time Erick had said words like that.

It didn't take Erick long to rig the safety rope along the primitive steps of the shaft. He had even brought a miner's hat with a light above his head. Fortunately, there was a strong hook attached to the outside of the retaining wall where the outside portion of the rope would be secured. When all was in place, Erick went over and kissed Maddie and told her not to worry. He was used to fixing things in the dark of night on the freighter deck. Glenn stood by the outside portion of the rope monitoring the hook and rope. Toby calmed down. All was silent as the group concentrated on Erick's descent into the shaft. Erick had also set up a walkie talkie so he could communicate with Glenn and Maddie. He began speaking into the walkie talkie.

"I'm half way down. There's nothing but dirt walls which seem to be in pretty good shape. The light above my forehead is working fine. I'm just about at the bottom of the shaft which I estimate to be at least twenty feet from the surface. I'm using my flashlight to check around.

It's dry down here. No sign of water. Wow, I see a box of some sort. It almost looks like a small safe except its shape is more like the shape of how a picture would be confined in it since it's thin, maybe four inches thick and about eight feet by eight feet. I'll need another rope down here so you can haul it up before you bring me up. I have some extra rope on the ground up there."

Glenn found the rope and threw one end down being careful to tie the other end to the clip on the retaining wall. Fortunately the clip was big enough to hold two thick pieces of roping.

"Thanks for the rope. I'm now tying it around the box which is encased in some sort of protective material, and it isn't that heavy. Okay, I think the box is secure, so Glenn you can start hauling away."

It was heavier then Glenn thought. Maddie came over to help. Even Toby, who was used to retrieving fowl during hunting season, took the end of the loop in his mouth and started pulling it back. Toby had a natural instinct for this. To him it was like recreation. Finally the box appeared at the top of the shaft and Toby was finally able to pull it through the opening. Glenn immediately took it from Toby's possession.

Next, Erick started his climb to the top of the shaft by pulling on the rope hand over hand. Climbing on the primitive rock steps reminded him of the days as a boy when he and his friends would go rock climbing. As Erick pulled himself out of the shaft, Maddie ran over threw her arms around him and whispered in his is ear, "I love you too." Releasing himself from the rope, he exclaimed, "Well let's see what it is." The group wanted to cheer but didn't want to draw attention to them or to the site.

Glenn suggested they open the box at his lodge. It would be safer there, but before taking it up it would be wise to shut the door to the shaft, and to pull the vines over so the door would be hidden, then they should remove all their tools and equipment.

There was such an air of excitement with adrenaline flowing that the clean up job took just a few minutes. By the time the group left for the lodge, the retaining wall had been totally covered by the vines appearing as if nothing had happened.

The group had just settled into the chairs and sofa around Glenn's fireplace when they heard a car pull up on the gravel road. It was the

Sheriff. Maddie and Erick immediately hid the package in one of the bedrooms.

"Remember," Erick said, "we can't talk to anyone about what we found, even the Sheriff."

Glenn greeted the Sheriff and invited him to join the group by the fire. The Sheriff initiated the conversation, "We've received some new information from the tests that were run on Ms. Kirkpatrick's Pasty. Using a strong magnifying glass our scientists found a prick in the crust that encircled the food inside the Pasty. It is the same size as a hypodermic needle from a shot just like one you would see in a doctor's office for vaccinations. The Pasty received a shot of arsenic. The entry point was microscopic so we almost missed it. We think that the guy who offered to deliver the Pasties for Johnny inserted the poison into the Pasty somewhere along the route between the Pasty shop and the construction site. We still don't have a lead on this person who is now wanted for attempted murder. So, Ms. Kirkpatrick, you still need to be very careful."

While listening to the Sheriff, Erick had a thought, "Sheriff, has the town of Munising or whatever jurisdiction the lighthouse property is in had meetings concerning this property and are there county or town regulations that apply to this property? Also, were there any town hearings on what, if any requirements should be put on the property after it was sold to a private person. In other words, how did the locals feel about Ms. Kirkpatrick buying then turning the property into a B&B?"

"Don't worry about that Mr. Dawson, we did have town meetings and the jurisdiction was unanimously enthusiastic about anyone who would fix up the property. With a B&B your property will add to our tourism. And now, if you have no more questions, I need to leave."

Thanking the Sheriff, the group breathed a sigh of relief. When all was clear Glenn brought out the mysterious box. Sitting around the fire, Maddie with the help of Erick gently opened the box and found a package. They opened the package as if it were a valuable Christmas gift by peeling away the several layers of protective cover. They finally saw their gift.

In front of them was an old painting—a very old painting. The scene was a farmer's field with an old barn in the foreground. There was a small farm house in the background in front of a forest to one side and a lake to the other side. Could the lake be Lake Superior? The lake did show waves with white caps. What could be so special about this? It was obvious there was not much value to it.

"There has to be something more to this then what we are actually seeing", Erick suggested.

Maddie thoughtfully added, "The only one around here who might be able to help us is Wilson. Wil said he is an art history major and so maybe he could shed some light on what this painting is all about and why it has been hidden more than twenty feet under the ground for all these years."

"But, Maddie and Erick, what about the secrecy of this?" Glenn asked.

Maddie answered, "Glenn, we will never know unless we can bring in a consultant and I think he'll try his best to keep the secret. After all, it is for our safety. So, where can we hide the painting tonight until we can get Wil over here?"

Glenn addressed Maddie and Erick, "Why don't you stay in one of my extra bedrooms, Maddie. I have a big safe in the den.

There is also a sofa sleeper in there, so Erick you can sleep there. It's very cozy, Erick, and you'll have your own fireplace. I have double locks on my doors and a security system will be alerted."

Erick suggested that he would go talk to Wil in the morning so as not to arose suspicion. Then, they could take a late morning break from their jobs and maybe combine it with their lunch break.

CHAPTER 30

Morning dawned bright and clear. The painting was still safely hidden in Glenn's safe and no one had seen or heard anything in Glenn's yard overnight. There hadn't been any sounds as if someone were tinkering with the door or the lock.

Their very kind host had already cooked a delicious breakfast of bacon and eggs, french toast and hot coffee made from locally grown beans. A silver bowel filled with a mixture of several kinds of fresh fruit graced the center of the table.

"Glenn, thank you so much for such a wonderful treat. Your breakfast is delicious. Are you sure you haven't been a chef at sometime in your life?" Maddie teased.

"Well, I was the chief cook at my house. My wife had many talents, but had no interest in cooking."

Erick was the first to finish breakfast.

"I'd better get an early start at the lighthouse so I can clue Wil in about our extended morning break. I'll see you back here around 11am."

Maddie began to clear the table.

"You're the chef, Glenn, so I'll be your dishwasher and will clean the kitchen for you."

Glenn smiled. In a way, Maddie reminded him of his late wife. He could also see that Maddie and Erick had more than just a fondness for each other and hoped that something would come of it. They made a great couple and complemented each other very nicely.

As Erick approached the lighthouse, he could see that Wil's car was already in the parking lot. Wil was inside working on the spiral steps.

"Morning, Wil. Would you be able to take an extended break with me at 11am? Maddie and I need your art expertise on something we found by the the keeper's house, but we need to keep this secret now for security purposes."

Wil immediately looked interested.

"Erick, I'm sure Brad will let me go. I'll just tell him you all need some help with something that has to do with the remodeling."

Wil was right. Brad had no hesitation in letting him go with Erick. In fact, Brad was so confident in Wil that he didn't even ask what it was about. After all, Wil was his nephew and he had known him all his life.

After finishing her work in the kitchen, Maddie grabbed another cup of coffee and decided to enjoy Glenn's porch on such a beautiful day. She enjoyed watching the activity around her property as the construction crew worked on connecting the breezeway to both the lighthouse and keeper's house.

The crew seemed to be excellent at multitasking. What she did't know was that someone else was also watching the progress of the construction from a secure hiding place very close by.

When she finally saw Erick and Wil walking towards Glenn's lodge, she felt a flutter of nervousness and excitement. Perhaps the painting would answer some questions or have clues to the strange occurrences within the last few weeks.

"Hi, Wil. We're so glad you could take some time off so we could show you what we found on the property."

Glenn came to the door to greet Erick and Wil.

"Why don't you all come in and we can sit around the fireplace and tell Wil what we're up to."

After they had settled in the living room, Glenn went to get the painting out of his safe, then handed it to Maddie who began the explanation.

"Wil, we found a door in the retaining wall which was hidden by the beautiful flowers draping over the wall. We were able to break the lock on the door. Behind the door was a shaft large enough for a man to go inside and descend to the bottom. There were some very rudimentary steps carved into the wall of the shaft. Erick was able to get to the bottom which was about twenty feet down. We found this painting wrapped very securely on the floor of the shaft. We have no idea how valuable it might be. We decided that since you're the art history student here you might be able to tell us something about it. And, before we go any further, please know that this is to be kept a secret. Only we four know about it. It's for security purposes."

Maddie then handed the painting to Wil. Without even glancing at the painting, Wil immediately turned the painting over, then explained, "You can learn more about a painting by looking at its back. Look here at the back of the canvas. I can tell it is very old as the back of the canvas is a dark beige. If it were light beige, it would be fairly new. But, yours is old and may even date back to the 1800's. I'm also looking at the open weave along the edges of its edge. As you can see, in this weave there is more room between the open holes which also tells me that it is an older painting and could be more valuable."

Wil then looked at the picture.

"The picture is not painted that well. Actually, it looks like a painting that wouldn't be in a museum but something you could have found in a flea market. However, there is a possibility that the picture is an 'over painting.'"

Maddie was startled.

"Wil, do you mean someone painted a different picture over the original."

Wil told her that is what overpainting was and most of it was done in the nineteenth century.

"Ms. Kirkpatrick, overpainting was done by artists if they wanted to correct something during the creation of the painting. Sometimes, it was done for security purposes to hide the original painting if they thought the painting was very valuable."

Wil went on to explain that during World War II when the Nazis started looting the valuables from the Jewish people. Those who had expensive art pieces would paint a simple picture over the expensive one, hoping the Nazis would think the picture had no value so wouldn't loot it.

"If you are interested, Ms. Kirkpatrick, I know of a gentleman who works at the Minneapolis Institute of Art. He is not only an appraiser but restores and conserves art. He would have all the tools needed to confirm the overpainting and would be able to remove the overpainting without hurting the original painting. Since we don't know the value of the painting, it should be locked in a very secure place. So, if you want to pursue this, I would call him now and you can set an appointment."

Maddie looked at Erick and they both nodded in agreement.

"I have his number in my phone, so I'll call him now then pass the phone over to you in order to make the appointment. His name is Nick Johnson."

Wil walked to the back of the room to make the call. He was put through to Nick and after chatting with Nick for a few minutes while explaining the situation, he returned to Maddie and handed her the phone. She made an appointment for two days later and was advised that if she flew to Minneapolis not to check the painting. If the painting was too large to carry on the plane, Nick suggested that they drive. It would be about a nine or ten hour drive.

Erick would definitely go with Maddie. As much as Maddie wanted Wil to go, it might arouse suspicion among the construction crew since he was supposed to be working full time for his uncle.

Maddie walked over to Wil and gave him a big hug and thanked him for his expertise.

"Erick and I will definitely take you and Glenn out for dinner when we return. You both have been so helpful."

After Wil had left to go back to the construction site, Maddie turned to Glenn.

"Can Erick and I impose on you for one more night."

"Of course you can. Toby and I like to have guests. So, give me your painting and I'll take it back to the safe."

Erick walked over to Maddie and putting his arm around her said in a low voice, "I think we should leave first thing in the morning. Driving would be safer and wherever we go, even into restaurants, the painting goes with us.

CHAPTER 31

As Maddie and Erick rolled their suitcases into the living room, Glenn appeared in the kitchen doorway and insisted they stay for a full breakfast before leaving. The aroma of the coffee and bacon tempted them to stay for Glenn's breakfast.

"You need more than a continental breakfast today since you have a long haul ahead of you. I'm guessing it is about ten hours. Do you think you'll make it in one day?"

"We'll try Glenn," Erick answered as he took a seat at the dining room table.

"But, we will have to eat fast."

Maddie added, "Don't forget, Erick, I have to stop at the inn in Sault Ste. Marie to get a few clothes and to check on Matt and Heidi. I hope when we get to Minneapolis, Nick Johnson will let us watch as he examines the painting."

As Glenn finished pouring cups of coffee for Maddie and Erick, he left for the kitchen, then to the den where he retrieved the painting from the safe.

"Here's your mysterious painting, Maddie. We've kept it safe and sound here. I can't wait to hear what the verdict is on its history and value."

"Yes, this should be interesting, Glenn. Thanks so much for your kindness in letting us stay with you, but we have to hit the road especially since we have to factor in stopping at the inn in Sault Ste. Marie."

"Just stay safe, you two, and I'll be waiting for your return."

The trip to Sault Ste. Marie was uneventful. The painting which had been carefully wrapped was placed on the back seat. Fortunately,

Maddie and Erick made the almost two hour trip to Sault Ste Marie without needing to stop.

"When we get to the inn, Maddie, I'll stay in the car with the painting while you go in to pack some more clothes and talk to Matt and Heidi. All car doors will be locked."

Both Matt and Heidi were checking out some guests so Maddie just waved at them and went to her small apartment in the back of the inn to pack some clothes. By the time she returned to the front desk, most of the morning guests had checked out. She told Matt and Heidi that she and Erick were driving to Minneapolis and had an appointment with a consultant concerning the lighthouse. She didn't dare mention the painting.

"Heidi and I can handle everything just fine, Maddie."

Maddie asked Matt to meet her in the back office.

"Thank you, Matt, for taking over while I am gone. Have you had any problems with Heidi such as her taking longer than usual lunches?"

"She's been doing just fine, Maddie. She does seem distracted though as if something is worrying her."

"As long as you can count on her, Matt, that should be okay. I may be gone for a few days so call me anytime if you need something, and I will try to stay in touch everyday. You'll earn a nice bonus for this when I return."

When Maddie returned to the car, Erick was studying the map.

"It looks like from here, we should take 75 south to Rt. 2 at St. Ignace then take that west to Rte. 41in Wisconsin down to Green Bay where we would hook up with 29W towards Minneapolis which turns into Rte. 94 right before the city of Minneapolis."

Erick further explained that the trip would take about ten hours and was around Five hundred fifty five miles away. If they took turns driving, they could drive straight through. And, since their appointment with Nick Johnson was in the afternoon, they could spend the night somewhere closer to Minneapolis like in Eau Claire, Wisconsin which was about an hour and a half from Minneapolis, or Wausau which was around three hours away from the city. The place closest to a half way point was Green Bay, a four and a half hour drive to Minneapolis and five hours from Sault Ste. Marie.

"Erick, why don't we see how we feel by the time we get to Greenbay. If we want the longest day to be today, I'd opt for a stop in Wausau for the night. It's only six and a half hours from the Sioux to Wausau."

As they pulled away from the Twin Sisters Inn, they didn't see a maroon colored car with tinted windows pull out of a street parking place, make a U-turn and begin to follow them.

Once on Rte. 75, their trip went very fast as of the higher Interstate speed limit. Arriving in St. Ignace, they turned onto Rte. 2 which would take them from Michigan into Wisconsin.

"One thing we have to remember, Erick, is to turn our watches back one hour when we arrive in Wisconsin. "Both Wisconsin and Minnesota are on central time so that gives us an extra hour today and we could make it to Wausau."

"Thanks for the reminder. Another idea to consider is that for our meals, we should only use drive-thru service so we don't have to leave the car and for bathroom breaks we go in one at a time so one of us is with the painting at all times in a locked car."

There weren't many cars on Rte 2 heading for Wisconsin. As Erick glanced in the rear view mirror, he saw the maroon car not far behind, but didn't think much about it until he came to one of the few major intersections on the mostly rural road. There was more traffic there. Erick had to stop for a red light and when it turned green, the maroon car followed after him straight through the light. A gnawing feeling began to grow as he glanced several more times in the in the rear view mirror. Were they being followed? He decided not to mention this to Maddie until he was sure.

"I'm going to stop at the next gas station to top off the tank. I haven't seen many stations out here so will take advantage of the first one we come to. Also, are you hungry for lunch?"

"Sure, I could go for a fast food burger and fries."

Maddie was still not aware of Erick's concern about being followed.

Finally, there was a sign for a gas station about four miles away. As they came to an intersection with only farmers' fields in sight, a little sign pointed to a gas station located two miles after a right turn. Erick turned right as did the maroon car. After what seemed to be much more than two miles, Erick saw a small gas station on the left. There was also a small country store behind it. Erick pulled in and drove to one of the gas pumps. The maroon car pulled in too but parked in front of the station's country store. When Erick's tank was full, he asked Maddie, "Would you like any snacks? I think I'll get some. This may be the only gas station for miles. just tell me what you want then lock the doors."

Erick glanced at the maroon car but couldn't see the person inside. He bought a couple of drinks, some chips, popcorn and candy. He hoped they would find a fast food restaurant within a few hours.

As soon as Erick returned to the car and pulled away from his spot at the pump, the maroon car also backed out. Erick turned right to head back to Rte. 2. Erick thought it was time to share his fears with Maddie.

"Now, my dear one, I don't want you to be nervous, but for the last couple hours or so a maroon car has been following us. I think I remember seeing it for the first time just outside of Sault St. Marie. He pulled into the gas station but didn't buy any gas or go into the store for anything."

"What are we going to do, Erick?"

"Nothing, but just continue on. Just to let you know, I came prepared. I have my gun and also the usual pepper spray. But, I'll keep watching to see how close he comes to us."

"Don't you think, Erick, that we should begin to watch for a fast food restaurant so we can get a late lunch at the drive-thru?"

Driving in the country was refreshing but lonely, especially since the maroon car was the only other car around. It was a welcome relief to see the 'Welcome to Wisconsin' sign. They turned off of Interstate 2 and onto 41 south to Greenbay. The maroon car followed them.

Erick suggested they get a late lunch or early dinner in Green Bay then continue on to Wausau where they could stay for the night. That way they would have only about a three hour drive to Minneapolis the next morning so they could get there, have lunch and be on time for their afternoon appointment with Nick Johnson.

"Don't forget, Maddie, we just entered Wisconsin so we're on central time and need to turn our watches back an hour."

As they got closer to Green Bay the area wasn't so rural. Instead, they passed through many small towns.

"Well, here we are in Green Bay Packer territory."

"Yeah, they are one of my favorite teams, Maddie."

As they got closer to Green Bay, a variety of fast food restaurants came into sight.

"So, what's you're choice, Maddie? McDonalds, Arbys or Burger King?"

"I think I'll take McDonalds. It has been a long time since I had their Quarter Pounder with cheese and fries. I would also love an iced tea with lemon."

As they turned into McDonalds, the maroon car followed them and stayed behind them at the drive-thru. When they had their food, Erick pulled into a parking space so they could eat in the car. Maddie left to go to the restroom. Erick watched her closely as she entered the restaurant. He was afraid the person in the maroon car would approach her. The maroon car had parked in another space. Within a few minutes, Maddie appeared at the side of their car and quickly got in.

"This is such an enjoyable treat. I've forgotten how delicious the quarter pounder is."

After they had finished, it was Erick's turn to visit the restroom.

"Maddie, when I leave, lock the doors immediately and don't put the window down to talk to anyone."

She kept her eyes on the maroon car. She didn't realize that the driver had also left his car to enter the restaurant. Suddenly, she saw the person, a man, leave the restaurant and while he walked to the maroon car, he kept his eyes on Eric's car. He wore sunglasses so Maddie couldn't see him well but he seemed to fit the description of the man Erick had followed from Canada to Sault Ste. Marie, Michigan, however, that man had a black car. Either way, just looking at him sent shivers down her spine.

When Erick returned, Maddie told him about seeing the man.

"Erick, he might have been in the restroom the same time you were."

"Yeah, and when I think of it, we should make a list of all the suspicious people we've seen since you bought the lighthouse."

"Well, Erick, there was the angry man at the auction and he appeared again at Ben's Book and Craft Store in Sault Ste. Marie. Then, there was the man Heidi met in Canada who then drove her back to the inn. You took a picture of them having lunch in the restaurant in Canada.

And now, there is this guy in the maroon car. And, don't forget, there was also the man who delivered the pasty to the lighthouse including mine that was poisoned. Then there was the person who hit Glenn over the head which knocked him out. That was even before we met him. So, do you think there is some sort of connection between them?"

"I don't know, but once Nick analyses the painting, we should tell him about these strange occurrences. He may have some ideas about why this could happen. They're just not strange occurrences anyway mainly because the attempted murder of you was planned since someone tried to poison you. Your life is in danger and I think there is something that goes much deeper than this painting."

When they pulled out of the McDonald's parking lot, Erick began looking for Rte. 29 which would take them to Wausau, and then onto Rte. 94 in the morning which was a direct route to Minneapolis.

"So, now that we're on Rte. 29, could you please use your Iphone to look for hotels? And guess who's still behind us?"

Maddie started looking for hotels. Wausau had the usual array of nice hotels—Hilton Garden Inn, Holiday Inn, Hampton Inn, and Courtyard by Marriott naming a few.

Most were close to Rte 29. She read the amenities to Erick who finally replied, "It's your choice."

"Well, my dear Erick, I think I'll choose Courtyard by Marriott. It sounds great and is not far from Rte 29. It is on 1000 S. 22nd. Ave."

The trip to Wausau was just under two hours. They arrived before dark. Erick was going to try to lose the maroon car by trying to get far ahead of the car then to take a quick exit to the hotel before the man could see where they exited. He saw the exit for 22nd Ave. was two miles ahead so he sped up and changed lanes quickly. The maroon car tried to keep up but was having difficulty due to the evening rush hour traffic. With a half mile to go, Erick saw the maroon car a few cars behind. At the last minute, he quickly changed to the right lane just before the bottom of the exit ramp. The maroon car hadn't been able to exit. Erick went right to the hotel and parked behind it then told Maddie to stay in the car with the doors locked. Erick jogged around to the front and entered. At the front desk he registered for two adjoining rooms for one night. He then found the back door to the hotel which led to the back parking lot.

At the car he told Maddie to get her overnight bag and he would carry the painting and his bag. They would enter by the back door in order to stay out of sight, then take the back elevator to their floor.

Once settled in their rooms, they kept the adjoining doors open. Erick suggested he keep the painting in his room next to his bed since if someone broke in, he had his gun. They both decided to order out and have the dinners delivered to their rooms. The hotel had a list of amenities including names of restaurants which would deliver meals. The meals even included a bottle of wine.

"Of course, Maddie, if we were true Wisconsinites we would order beer and brats which are very good here."

Their rooms were at the back of the hotel and overlooked the parking lot behind the hotel. From time to time, Erick would look out his window to see if the maroon car was parked there, but so far the maroon car was no where to be seen.

They ordered from a nearby Italian restaurant. Remembering what had happened with the Pasty delivery at the lighthouse, Erick had a creeping fear that if the man from the maroon car had found them, he could hijack the delivery man and offer to deliver the food for the delivery guy from the restaurant. So, when there was a knock on the door, Erick scrutinized the delivery man through the peephole. He was definitely Italian looking and when Erick opened the door the guy had a thick Italian accent. Erick thanked him and gave him a generous tip.

The rest of the evening was quiet and enjoyable. The wine relaxed them, and after such a stressful day, they retired early to their rooms and kept the adjoining doors to their rooms open for safety. They decided to leave by 8:30 am the next morning.

CHAPTER 32

At eight thirty the next morning Maddie, Erick and their painting drove out of the hotel to finish the trip to Minneapolis. They figured it would take about three hours so they would have enough time to find a hotel and have lunch before meeting Nick Johnson.

Their time projections were fairly accurate. By one pm they had checked into another Marriott hotel, and had grabbed a quick lunch at a nearby cafe. At two pm they entered the Minneapolis Instiue of Art. The receptionist called Nick Johnson to inform him of their arrival. He said he would meet them in the lobby. Within a matter of minutes Nick Johnson, a middle aged man with a very kind looking face, black hair and a little overweight, crossed the lobby to introduce himself.

"I hope you had a safe drive to Minneapolis. So, why don't we go to my lab. I would really prefer that you witness my work as I examine your painting. I'll try to explain what I am doing every step of the way. I would have loved to see Wil but I guess he had to stay because of his job. I was his mentor for a long time. He's a great kid and student."

Maddie immediately liked Nick and felt confident that he would give them good advice.

As they left the lobby conversing with each other, they couldn't have seen the maroon car which pulled up to the Institute then move a half block down the street to park out of sight.

Nick's lab was quite spacious. There were paintings of all sizes and in different stages of being examined. Nick led his guests to a large table in a corner which gave them more of a private feeling. There were some portable dividers that he moved to surround the area in order to keep the painting out of sight. Then came the big reveal. Maddie with the help of

Erick removed the painting from its packing materials which had kept it safe during the trip. Laying it carefully on the table, Nick quickly gazed at the picture then did what Wil had done. He turned the painting over to inspect the frame, check for a hidden signature or any other markings that could give him some clues. Like Wil, he suspected the painting was very old.

Nick then carefully removed the frame and looked under the area hidden beneath the frame.

"This is what we call the tacking edge. I am trying to uncover pigments which are light and clear because it will help me see the true color scheme of the underpainting."

Nick was using an ultra violet light because varnish-like shellac would create colored luminosity when subjected to the UV light.

"I've discovered a layer of varnish so I'm going to use a solvent on a cotton swab and by gently rubbing it I hope to open a window to display the true color beneath. This way we can discover the original color palette by the artist."

Nick was using a magnifying glass and a microscope using different lights. He was making notes and taking photographs.

"As you can see, this is a painstaking process. As a conservator, I have no margin for error since any loss is irrevocable."

Maddie was fascinated and asked, "So, Nick what type of training or degree did you get in order to be a conservator?"

"Most conservators, Ms. Kirkpatrick, have degrees in chemistry. I also have a second degree in material science so I can address a painting's structural problems."

"By the way, Ms. Kirkpatrick, how and where did you find this painting?"

Maddie explained how they found the secret door in the retaining wall and the hole in the ground.

"How deep was the hole?"

Erick answered, "It was at least twenty feet deep with rudimentary steps carved or built into the wall of the shaft. I was able to descend to the bottom where I found the painting which was securely wrapped and in a box."

Nick replied, "That tells me a lot. The person who dug the hole just to hide the painting must have known about the value of the painting. After you get to beyond ten feet, you have a steady temperature of around mid fifties in degrees, like 55 or 58 degrees. No matter how harsh the weather is above the ground, paintings will do well in their environment of fifty degrees or so. In fact in World War II when the European countries were bracing for the invasion of the Nazis, particularly in London, the museums packed all their paintings and hid them in secret caves or caverns in the countryside since caves maintain this steady temperature. In the other European countries such as France, the museums also hid their paintings in caves."

Maddie had a thought and a question:

"Nick, did Wil ever tell you anything about his family's background, especially about his family's hero named, Joey, who died in World War II."

"I knew that part of his family was Jewish and some relatives tried to flee Europe. But, I also know that, according to historical accounts, many of the Jewish people were very successful in their careers and earned good salaries. They were upper middle class and worked for the government or for private industry, and many had their own businesses.

Because of this, they had many valuables such as art, jewelry and antiques which were stolen by the Nazis. So, Ms. Kirkpatrick, you might try to probe a bit more into Wil's family background if he'll let you particularly if you want to know the history of the painting."

By 6pm Nick informed Erick and Maddie that he wouldn't be able to finish his work on their painting until the next day, but had a safe where he could store it.

"I'm sure I'll have a decision for you tomorrow and hope to have the painting cleaned up enough so we can see the original underpainting. Why don't you come back tomorrow morning by 10 am."

"Nick, you must be tired, and we'd love to treat you to dinner tonight. Do you have a special restaurant in the area?" Erick asked.

"Thank you so much, but I can't do it tonight, but maybe before you leave. I can recommend a restaurant down the street that you'd probably enjoy. It's a very good Swedish restaurant called the Scandi Kitchen. It has a delicious smorgasbord or as they say in Swedish, 'a buttered table.' The variety of fish, meats, vegetables and sweets is phenomenal."

Erick thanked him.

"That sounds delicious to us, so we'll be on our way and will see you tomorrow morning."

As Erick and Maddie entered the restaurant, they were impressed with how cozy the atmosphere was. Small booths were placed around the perimeter of the room. The huge and attractive buffet table in the center displayed so many delectable offerings, it was going to be hard to decide what to choose.

As the waitress explained that there was one price for the smorgasbord. She then suggested that before going to the smorgasbord, they should try some of their famous Swedish glow mulled wine. Although it was a traditional Christmas treat, she said they served it all year especially for their tourists. It was made of red wine with cinnamon, orange and cloves, raisons, vodka and cognac and was heated. The wine was already prepared and within a few minutes the waitress appeared with two steaming mugs, and as she placed them in front of Erick and Maddie, she added, "This will for sure relieve the stress from your day. And, feel free to go to the smorgasbord and choose whatever you wish. You can return as many times as you like." After a few sips of the delicious warming drink, Maddie and Erick decided to take a trip around the smorgasbord table. Maddie tried some of the pickled herring which in Swedish style had a less sharp, and sweeter taste than in the rest of Europe due to its sweet brine. Erick chose smoked mackerel and a small piece of a commonly known fish called 'Arctic Charr.' Of course, there were also Swedish meatballs served with Ligonberry jam and boiled or mashed potatoes. Looking at the reindeer and the the bear sausage, they were not sure if they had the courage to taste it, but each put a small sample on their plates. As they ate, they gazed around the room observing the Viking theme. There were pictures of Norsemen and Viking ships on the North Sea which were beautifully framed and hung attractively on the dark green walls.

Just as they were thinking of taking another round at the table for desserts, the front door of the restaurant opened and a man walked in. He was greeted by the hostess and as she was showing him to his booth, Erick, who was facing the front door, looked up and gasped silently.

"What' wrong Erick."

"Don't turn your head Maddie, but a guy just came in and I got a pretty good look at him when the hostess was showing him to a booth. I could swear he is the man I saw with Heidi at the restaurant in Sault. Ste. Marie, Canada."

Erick quickly took his camera from his back pocket and flipped through the pictures trying to find the one he had taken of Heidi and the man while they were sitting at their table in the restaurant.

"Wow, I think he's the same man."

Erick turned the camera around to show Maddie.

"Do you think he is the one from the maroon car that has been following us?"

"I think so, but in Canada he had a black car, but maybe he rented this car."

Erick wondered if the man had seen him and Maddie when they entered the restaurant.

"As I said, Erick, maybe he rented this car because it is a different color than the one you saw in Canada. If that is so, it probably means that he knows you saw him in Canada."

"Maddie, we're going to have to be very careful and vigilant while we're here in the city. I think the danger has followed us here from the Shipwreck coast and from Sault Ste. Marie."

"Erick, why don't we go back to the smorgasbord table and survey the desserts, then choose one and ask the waitress to box our desserts for us so we can take them back to the hotel. That way while we are at the smorgasbord table, we can take our time and hopefully get a few glances at the guy."

Erick felt tempted to confront the man while he had a chance and was in a public place, but then he thought better of it.

Taking their time at the smorgasbord table one last time, they saw a variety of cakes, many of which were made with a cinnamon flavor. There were also cinnamon buns some of which were spiced with cardamon, a spice the Vikings first brought back from Constantinople or what is today, Istanbul. There was Norwegian almond cake made with heavy cream and almond extract, Blackberry-Ginger pie, cranberry and lemon pies, apple and berry pies with homemade custard, Finnish tarts,

Norwegian cinnamon thumbs, Gelatin, Mazarin torte and Chocolate and Oat treats.

Maddie chose a Finnish tart and the apple and berry pie with homemade custard. Erick chose a traditional cinnamon bun and the blackberry-ginger pie.

They went to the far end of the table opposite the booth where the man was seated. Both took short quick glances at the man while they were looking at the desserts and trying to signal the waitress so they could show her which desserts they wanted to take with them in a box. They finally got her attention, and after she had come to the dessert portion of the table, she took the samples to prepare them in a box for carry out. They then returned to their booth following a route that went past the man's booth. His head was down and he appeared to be reading a newspaper while he sipped his drink. Even so, Erick was sure he was the same man who he had followed across the International Bridge to the United States.

Trying to act very nonchalant, Erick and Maddie checked their desserts in the box, paid for their dinner and left. As they walked towards their car even though it was dark, they both glanced around the lot to see if there was a maroon car there. There was no maroon car. Once they got into their car, in order to return to the hotel, they had to pass the Scandi Kitchen, go to the next light and make a U-turn. Just a couple blocks from the restaurant, and before the traffic light, there it was—the maroon car parked on the street.

"Did that man in the restaurant look familiar to you, Maddie?"

"No, I've never seen him before and where I sat at the Scandi, I sat with my back to him."

"So, this means we are rapidly consolidating our list of people who have a huge interest in the painting. At least he hadn't left the restaurant before we got to the light and made a U-turn. I hope he doesn't know where we are staying."

"I wouldn't be so sure about that, Erick. I'll bet he knows where we are."

Chapter 33

The heated mulled wine with the filling Swedish meal worked wonders on relaxing Erick and Maddie. Again, they had adjoining rooms and kept the common door open for safety. Sleep came rapidly and gently when they finally retreated to their beds.

Breakfast at the hotel's cafe in one end of the lobby the next morning was another relaxing. way to wake up. They didn't have to meet Nick until 10 am and the Art Institute was close by.

They decided to check out of the hotel in order to try to throw the man off their trail. If Nick's work took most of the day, they would begin to drive back and find a hotel on the way.

At 10am sharp they entered the Art Institute. The receptionist told them to go immediately to Nick's lab. As they entered, they saw Nick concentrating so hard on gently removing the rest of the varnish of the over painting that he did not hear, so they knocked lightly on the open door to alert him but not to startle him. He was wearing a jeweler's head-mounted visor with a small light on it.

"Come in, I'm making a lot of progress on this and I don't think it will take all day."

He then turned to them and nervously asked if they had heard about the incident the night before. Erick and Maddie said that they had heard nothing. He continued, "After I left and the museum was locked for the night, someone broke in. We have a state of the art alarm system here, but somehow they disconnected it. The door to my lab was double locked and fortunately when I started working here, I insisted they replace the window in my hall door with the type of glass that can't be broken. Most people don't know about that kind of glass, but I have a friend who secures buildings and he recommended it. Anyway, your painting was secure as it was locked in the vault."

Maddie asked, "Nick, what time did this happen last night?"

"About forty five minutes after you left and I left right after you did, then immediately after, the Institute was locked down and the alarms turned on."

Becoming more curious, Erick asked, "Does this happen very often here?"

"No, Erick, this has never happened ever since I've been here."

Looking up from his work with an anxious look on his face, Nick added, "In the last few months there have been some attempted robberies in other museums. We think there might be some kind of a coordinated theft ring stealing art and valuables from museums in this city and nearby towns. The Institute already has called someone in from the art and antiquities division of the FBI."

As Nick continued with his work on the painting, Erick recounted how he and Maddie had been followed by a maroon car all the way to Minneapolis from Sault Ste. Marie, then we were followed last night to the Scandi Kitchen.

"But, last night the guy from the maroon car came in to eat about an hour after we arrived there. I think I recognized him from another incident where I saw him in Sault St. Marie, Canada."

"Maybe you should report him to the FBI here. The FBI came in this morning to talk to the curator of the Institute, and his contact information is at the desk in the lobby."

Chills went down Maddie's back. A theft ring particularly working in many cities and states would have contacts all over the country and perhaps in Europe or Central and South America, and also in Canada just north of Minneapolis. How could she keep them from knowing everything thing she did or everywhere she went. At least she had the love of her life, Erick, with her. She knew he felt the same.

"Nick, Eric and I would like to meet with the FBI agent before we leave."

"Why don't you call now for an appointment. Maybe he would come over here. We all could meet in the lab, and that way the man who was following you wouldn't know we were all meeting as he probably would if you drove to the FBI."

Maddie immediately left for the front desk to ask for the FBI contact information. Once on the line, she was put through to Dan Ford, the agent who visited the Institute. She peeked his curiosity and he agreed to meet the group in Nick's lab within the hour.

Dan Ford was a very pleasant, but also very serious agent. He was of medium height and wore the typical FBI dark suit with white shirt, and conservative looking tie. After introductions, Maddie explained her situation beginning with the lighthouse auction in Duluth where she acquired both the lighthouse and keeper's house on the Shipwreck Coast. She explained the strange situations which happened including the attempt on her life with a poisonous Pasty.

Dan Ford interrupted, "So, how did you come into possession of the painting?"

"We found it buried in a twenty foot shaft.. The entrance to the shaft was hidden by flowers cascading over a retaining wall on my property." She explained.

"What led you to that spot, Ms. Kirkpatrick?"

"Erick and I figured someone was searching for something that might be valuable which probably would be somewhere on my property. So, I began a search of the property grounds then intended to search the lighthouse and keeper's house."

Then, Agent Ford asked her how she knew there was any value to the painting.

Maddie told him that one of the construction workers is an Art History major and studies paintings. When he examined her painting, he was sure that it had been overpainted and since Nick Johnson had been his mentor, he referred Maddie to Nick.

Turning to Nick Johnson, Agent Ford asked, "Mr. Johnson, as you are working on the painting now, what are you finding?"

"Mr. Ford, I'm very sure this is an overpainting. I've only gotten to the point where I can see portions of the painting underneath. My thought is someone painted over it to protect the real painting which I am guessing could be very valuable. The back of the painting as I explained to Erick and Ms. Kirkpatrick shows the frame to be very old, perhaps eighty years or more. I have a sneaking suspicion the painting could be a product of the 1800's or older."

The FBI agent watched as Nick continued removing the overpainting, then he added, "You may not know that we at the FBI have the National Stolen Art File which is online. It has been very helpful in two ways. Art has been entered into the National Stolen Art File since 1979. Then, secondly, the National Stolen Art File has generated a lot more interest in art theft plus in due diligence for the collectors, art dealers, and others who are involved in selling art or just looking for art for themselves. After checking the file, if they have a problem or question about a piece of art they can contact us and we'll help them resolve it by following leads. The head of our art theft program helps us by locating art experts for us such as someone like Nick.."

As Nick worked, Dan Ford continued to explain that arresting the bad guys is a secondary focus because if the bad guys know the FBI is closing in, they might try to destroy the valuable work. So, if they're afraid they'll get caught, the painting they might destroy could be worth millions. Thus the primary mission of the art team is to keep the painting safe.

"Agent Ford, do you just specialize in paintings?" Maddie asked.

"No, Ms. Kirkpatrick, we also work with all cultural property which includes sculptures, antiquities, books, manuscripts, coins, rock and roll memorabilia, jewelry, and even a pair of ruby slippers worn by Judy Garland in the 1939 movie, "The Wizard of Oz." They were worth millions."

Dan Ford also explained that an even larger part of their portfolio was investigating fraud cases which involve fakes and forgeries of all materials that he had just described. Then he addressed Nick, "You're doing such a great job here. Have you ever considered joining the FBI in the arts and antiquities division?"

Nick smiled.

"I'll think about it but I kind of like my own lab here at the Art Institute."

Gently wiping the last piece of the overpainting off, the group stood back to see what they had. What they saw was beautiful and breathtaking. In front of them was a painting depicting a snowy path through the middle of a forest of tall evergreen trees on either side. It was nighttime and people dressed in nineteenth century clothing were walking along the path towards a bright light in the distance. It depicted hope in the middle of darkness. The nighttime sky was lit up by a huge orange moon. Every few feet there were small late fall flowers on either side of the path. The women were carrying baskets of fruits and flowers as if they had been to a market somewhere outside of the woods. In the background and barely visible were small forest creatures watching the women but not making a sound except for a little rustling.

Nick turned the painting over and with a magnifying glass tried to find an artist's signature. He found a very faint signature which seemed like a Dutch name. Turning back to the group, "I'm not sure of the exact value of the painting. But, here is what I know. First, the painter is probably from the Netherlands or from Germany. He is not one of the masters, but someone who was very popular locally at that time. Popularity can add to the price. I don't know who owned it previously but maybe Wilson Hall can help you with that. If he finds them he could check with the previous owners to see if they have any of the receipts or documentation. You can also double check with another appraiser from another museum."

"Second, I am now turning the painting over to check its condition."

Again, under a sharp light and with his magnifying glass Nick carefully went over the picture to check for rips or tears or cracks. Even though very old, the paint had not faded most probably due to being stored underground. The painting was in very good condition considering its age.

Third, the painting portrayed figures walking through the woods wearing red coats. Although the figures were small, their coats lent additional feelings to the painting. Nick said that some or lots of red in a painting could make it more valuable.

Fourth, Although the painting was small, but not too small, Nick mentioned that it will still be noticed hanging on a wall as it exudes what is called 'wall power' but does not command the room.

Nick then turned to the group and said, "For a small painting, I think this one is valuable and if you can discover more of the history as to who owned it previously, and did it come from Europe, it would be very valuable. I would say at least a half a million dollars."

Maddie and Erick gasped. Then turning to Agent Ford, Maddie added, "I was planning on framing the picture and hanging it in the keeper's house, but if it is so valuable, should I even consider that?"

"Ms. Kirkpatrick, if you want to display it as it should be, there are always very safe display cabinets on the market."

Then Nick added, "Our museum or any other museum could suggest the best and safest display cabinets and where you can buy them and also find an expert to install them."

Dan Ford turned to Maddie again and to her surprise informed her that although he worked out of the Minneapolis office, his territory also extended to Michigan especially to the Upper Peninsula.

"Ms. Kirkpatrick, your life is still in danger. Now that we know the potential value of the painting, whatever group is behind this will eventually find out. So, I have decided to ask for a temporary transfer to Sault Ste. Marie until we catch the thieves. Our FBI branch is in Marquette, Michigan and that is about three hours from Sault Ste. Marie. I'm sure for this case I can obtain permission to open up a small branch office in or near Sault Ste. Marie. Our work is not over yet and I will need to continue to meet with you and Erick."

Maddie felt so relieved to know that Agent Ford would be in town and to have Erick staying with her in the inn.

Thanking Nick for his work, Dan Ford said goodbye to everyone and left.

"So, Nick, Maddie and I would like to take you out to dinner to thank you for all you have done for us. Where would you like to go?"

"Thanks, Erick. There's a little Italian restaurant two doors down. I'll lock the painting in the vault, then we can head over there."

The comradeship and delicious food and wine ended the evening on a positive note. Another suggestion from Nick was that Maddie could find more information from Wilson Hall and his family particularly those family members who had to flee Holland during World War II. This could give her a deeper insight into the painting.

After dinner, they returned to Nick's lab where they retrieved the painting from the vault.

They hugged and pledged to keep in touch then left Nick to lock up the lab while Erick and Maddie departed for their hotel. At all times the painting was in Erick's position.

Erick and Maddie headed out of Minneapolis intending to drive a couple of hours before stopping at a hotel. As darkness set in, a light rain began to fall. With the glare of the oncoming traffic it was becoming difficult to see the lane markings. Most of the traffic was slowing to half of what the speed limit allowed. After an hour on the road, they had only gone about twenty miles and the weather conditions were worsening. Seeing an advertisement for a Holiday Inn at the next exit, both of them decided it wasn't worth the effort to continue. So, Erick took the next exit. Fortunately, there were rooms at the hotel.

CHAPTER 34

Erick and Maddie left the Holiday Inn early in the morning hoping to get to the Twin Sisters Inn late that evening.

"Erick, how are we going to keep the painting safe once we get back? I have a safe at the inn but I don't think there is enough room for it.."

"Would you feel okay, Maddie, if Glenn kept it for us in his safe until we figure out where it should be permanently? We could also check what safe deposit boxes are available at the bank in Munising."

"First of all, Erick, it would be very late if we stopped at Glenn's lodge and we would still have over an hour drive to the Twin Sisters Inn. I know Glenn would be happy to keep it in his safe. However, since we now know the value of the painting, I think it might put Glenn in danger. There probably is someone who is watching us around the clock so real harm could come to the person who is taking care of the painting."

"Yes, and speaking of danger, I haven't seen the maroon car lately but that person surely knows we are returning to the Shipwreck Coast or Sault Ste. Marie. Since he knows our business in Minneapolis is finished, he'll be waiting for us when we return."

"Who would have thought, Erick, that finding a treasure like this could bring such fear and danger."

Maddie knew that her next step after finding a secure place for the painting would be to ask Wil if she could meet his parents so they could tell her about their relatives who had tried to flee the Nazis during World War II. She had a strange feeling that there was way more to the story of the painting then she had imagined, then she had a second thought.

"Erick, I'm rethinking this a bit. If you notice the rain is starting again which will delay us further, and I've always been afraid for Glenn since our enemy knows we're all so close. I think we should drop by the lodge and check on him and go back to the hotel in Munising."

At 10pm Erick parked in front of Glenn's lodge. He could see his lights were still on, so Maddie and Erick took the painting up to his door and rang the bell. Toby barked as Glenn opened the door.

"Please come in. I'm so glad you're safe and sound."

Toby excitedly sniffed everyone including the painting. When they were all seated in front of the fireplace, Maddie gave a brief version of their journey and what had been uncovered. She asked Glenn if they could keep their painting in his safe until they could find a more suitable place hopefully the next day.

"You can keep it here as long as you want, Maddie."

"Thank you so much, Glenn, but we think it would be too dangerous for you if we left it here for a long time. We now know there is someone or maybe a group who will stop at nothing to steal it."

"Don't worry, Toby, as friendly as he is, makes a great guard dog. He and I have been to training for that. But, I hope we don't have to see him in action."

"Well, Erick and I are staying at the hotel in Munising tonight so will be nearby and you have the number so don't hesitate to call at anytime."

Since they didn't have the painting with them when they left Glenn's house, Erick and Maddie decided to splurge and go to a bar in Munising near the hotel. The bar also served hamburgers and fries.

As they pulled into the parking lot, they could see that it must be busy as there were so many cars it was difficult to find a parking space. Walking towards the front door, Maddie glanced over to one side of the parking lot. A street light lit up the far side of the lot. Directly under the light Maddie saw the maroon car. She grabbed Erick's arm.

"Look at that!"

"This is a great chance, Maddie. Do you have a piece of paper. Let's go get the license plate number."

Rushing over to the car, they looked in the car, but even with the street light near the car, they could not see through the tinted windows.

Erick wrote down the license number. They then returned to the front door of the bar and entered hoping they would see a familiar face.

"We're going to the Sheriff's office in Munising tomorrow, Maddie, to find out who owns the car."

CHAPTER 35

Erick woke early in the morning. He was eager to get to the police station in order to report to the Sheriff that the maroon car was in town.

At 9am he arrived at the police station in Munising and was informed that the sheriff had been on travel for the last week. His lieutenant spoke with him. When Erick told him the story and showed him the license plate number, the lieutenant glanced at it then informed Erick the license plate number showed that the license plate number was a rental.

"Mr. Dawson, if you want to find out who rented the car, you will need to check with the rental agencies in the area. However, they may not give you the name of the renter due to privacy concerns."

"Lieutenant, how do you know this is a rental?"

"Because, Mr. Dawson, if you had looked closer you would have seen the barcode stickers on the windshield and/or the rear window. They scan the rental car as it goes out of the rental parking lot in order to keep track of it. Sometimes the dealer has its own license plate frame or has a plate that is painted the color of the fleet, or the car could sport a shiny new license plate covered with bar codes."

"If you want, I can print out all the nearby rental agencies within a twenty mile radius of this town. You could call and just ask of they have a maroon car in their fleet."

Erick left with the list of rental agencies knowing that they had a morning of phone calls ahead of him. He surmised that the car they had seen the night before at the bar parking lot was probably the car, but with a different renter.

Before he arrived at the hotel, his phone rang.

"Where have you been this morning, Erick? I had a great breakfast and am ready to continue our investigation."

He told Maddie that they should spend the morning calling the car agencies.

"But Erick, what will we do if we find the man?"

"We will figure that out when the time comes."

They divided the list of companies then went to their separate rooms to begin the phone marathon. By noon both Erick and Maddie had found two agencies that had a maroon car.

Both dealers were amenable to meeting with them.

After a quick lunch at the hotel cafe, they drove to the first dealership about ten miles out of town. The first dealer greeted them then led them through his parking lot to a maroon car. It resembled the car which had followed them, and the dealer's records showed that it had been rented during the time they had been on the road.

"Can you tell us anything about the person who rented the car?"

The dealer provided a description of a young man in his thirties, but informed them that he couldn't release the man's name. He had to protect the privacy of his clients. The only way they could learn of his identity would be through the police who would have to issue a warrant. He gave them his card and offered to call them if he thought of any other information.

The next rental lot put Erick and Maddie through the same procedure. The maroon car was a twin to the other car at the previous agency, however, the driver was different. The agent described the renter as a middle aged man. He was quite large in stature, very well built as if he worked out a lot. The agent also noticed that he was carrying a gun which was very secure in its holster.

"We usually don't see someone carrying a gun, but this is an open carry state so there was nothing we could question. Our records showed that when this person drove the car, he must have left the area and possibly the state since he had put a lot of miles on the car in a short period of time.""

Erick asked when the man had returned the car and the agent said he returned on the same day that Erick and Maddie had arrived at the hotel. The agent then informed them that after its return, the agency had cleaned the car immediately as another customer wanted it that night.

"Oh, and one more thing, the guy was dressed in jeans and a red plaid shirt. He also wore one of those white stetson cowboy hats. I also had a funny feeling as if I had seen him before but not at this dealership, but in the news. Maybe I saw him in the newspaper or on the television news. He seemed so familiar although I had never met him."

Trying not to jump to conclusions, Erick and Maddie thought the guy described by this rental agent was very close to whom they thought was following them. Maybe he was a local person.

They thanked the rental agent and left to retrieve their painting from Glenn's house. The sooner the better, they thought, as anyone in possession of the painting would be in danger and Maddie and Erick thought very highly of Glenn and appreciated his help throughout the search but were afraid for his safety.

"Hey, you two, how was your search? Did you find any more clues?"

Erick related the story about seeing the maroon car in the parking lot of the bar, and how they had found two maroon cars at different rental lots in the morning but weren't able to identify them.

"We're now going directly to a bank in Munising to rent a safety deposit box for the painting. What could be safer than a bank. And, Maddie needs to call her insurance agent to take out a special policy or rider on her policy which deals with valuables."

Glenn left the room to get their painting out of his vault. Upon his return, he handed it to Maddie and looking straight into her eyes cautioned, "You keep yourself safe. I don't want anything to happen to my new neighbor. Let me know if there is anything else I can do for you."

"Thanks, Glenn. You are so special to Erick and me."

Then, patting Toby's head as he looked up at her, she said, "You too are special Toby so keep Glenn safe."

The largest bank in town was The National Bank, so Maddie and Erick inquired about safe deposit boxes and were shown several sizes. The painting fit safely into the largest size. They had to rent it for a year which gave them more time than they needed, but at least they could relax knowing it was safe, and had enough time to figure out where it could permanently and safely be displayed.

Leaving the bank, they felt free for the first time in a long time, free from having to carry the painting around.

As they walked down the streets of Munising gazing in the display windows of the stores, they came to a small cafe. The lunch menu was posted on the window. It was the typical American fare. Of course, there were Pasties, but Maddie was still not ready to eat one yet. The thought of one made her stomach churn.

"Erick, after lunch, I'm going back to the hotel to call my insurance agent. I'll tell him what Nick told us and hopefully he can figure out how much insurance we'll need. Then, before returning to Sault Ste. Marie, I'm going to ask Wil if I can schedule a meeting with his parents as he mentioned that he had relatives who fled Nazi Germany during World War II, and I have a hunch there may be some clues in their story which could lead us to who might have been the last owner of the painting."

"While you do that, Maddie, I'll go back to help at the construction site."

Back in her room, Maddie dialed the number for The Northern Insurance Company. She asked for her agent, Mike Thresher.

"Good afternoon, Maddie. How are you? It's been quite a while."

"Hi, Mike. I have some exciting news for you. I've bought a lighthouse and its keeper's house and am turning them into a bed and breakfast."

She continued to explain most of the events which had happened, and what Nick Johnson at the Art Institute thought the value should be.

"So, I guess you're looking to buy some insurance to cover your valuable painting and the two buildings. I would suggest you get an additional appraisal and I can refer you to someone, but that would require taking your painting out of the safe deposit box and driving it to another museum. You would again be endangering yourself. However, there may be a way I can have the appraiser I know come to your bank in order to look at the painting. Most banks will give you a locked room so you and the appraiser can look at the painting. He would probably have to bring his tools he uses in appraisals."

Maddie asked Mike if she should wait to buy insurance until the second appraisal was done.

"You can take out a policy today, Maddie and it can be adjusted up or down after the second appraisal."

"Mike, I'd feel safer doing that. Since Nick thought the value was at least $ 500,000.00, I will take that amount out now. Is that a special type of policy since it covers a very valuable item?"

Mike explained that it would be a special policy from the policies on the two buildings.

Mike's office was located in Sault Ste. Marie, and since it was already 3:30pm, she decided on a morning appointment the next day at 10 am. She then finished her packing, checked out of the hotel and left for the construction site to talk to Wil.

Finding him working in the keeper's house, she asked Wil if he could take a break.

"I'll check with Brad. I'm supposed to have a break so I'm sure he'll let me take it now."

Wilson returned and told Maddie he had about fifteen minutes. She asked him if she could phone his parents to talk about their relatives who had fled Nazi Germany during World War II.

It was all about learning the history of a painting she had.

"Do you know my parents live in Duluth?"

"Yes, Wil and I would be happy to fly there or I would invite them to stay at my Twin Sisters Inn in Sault Ste. Marie or whatever would be easier for them."

Wilson gave Maddie their phone number and address in Duluth and told her their names were Carolyn and Doug Hall.

"Thanks, Will, you have been a tremendous help."

She then found Erick who was working on the staircase in the lighthouse to say she was leaving for Sault Ste Marie and would see him for dinner.

CHAPTER 36

Another sunny morning dawned in Sault Ste. Marie. Maddie had finished breakfast long before she saw Erick heading for the breakfast room.

She checked in with Matt and Heidi at the front desk. Business was normal as usual. There had been no problems while she was out of town which made Maddie breathe a sigh of relief since she felt as though she had been ignoring her employees and was concerned they might feel taken advantage of. Matt, however, did tell her discreetly that after work he did see that Heidi was picked up by someone in a black car. Both Matt and Maddie figured she must have a connection or relationship with someone but wished to keep it secret.

As she opened the door to her apartment in the inn, the phone was ringing and when Maddie answered, the voice at the other end asked to speak to Madeline Kirkpatrick.

"This is she, and who am I speaking to please?"

"This is Tom Holder. I am an appraiser of arts and artifacts and was referred to you by Mike Thresher."

"Oh, it's nice to hear from you. I'm so glad you called. I have a painting, but it is located in a vault in a bank in Munising. I have just returned to Sault Ste. Marie. Perhaps we could meet tomorrow afternoon which will give me time to drive back to Munising. The painting is at The National Bank in that town."

"That would be fine Ms. Kirkpatrick. I'll see you then around 2pm tomorrow."

Maddie's next phone call was to Carolyn and Doug Hall in Duluth, Minnesota. Carolyn Hall answered the phone and Maddie introduced herself and Carolyn Hall responded, "My son Wilson is working on the reconstruction of your lighthouse. He really enjoys doing that type of work and says your crew is very friendly.

Maddie explained that she had found a painting on the property and her son, Wil, had helped her in examining the painting, then referred her to an appraiser at the Minneapolis Insitute of Art.

"But, Carolyn, I'm trying to trace the history of the painting and would like to make an appointment with you and your husband since Wil told me that you had relatives in World War II who fled Nazi Germany. So, if it is okay with you, I would love to talk to you about your family's history."

"We would love to meet with you, Maddie. Would you like to visit us in Duluth?"

"Yes, I could come to Duluth, or I invite you to be my guest at my Twin Sisters Inn in Sault Ste. Marie. What would be more convenient for you?"

"I'll have to talk to Doug, but will get back to you in the next few days.. Doug works so it may be easier for you to come here. Anyway, we'll get this worked out very soon."

"Thanks so much, Carolyn. I look forward to hearing from you."

As Maddie walked back down the hall towards the lobby, she saw Erick leave the breakfast room.

"Erick", she called in a loud voice. She put her hand up for him to stop.

"Erick, we need to go somewhere private. I have something to tell you. Let's go to my apartment since the maids won't be cleaning in there until all the guests rooms have been cleaned."

As they sat in her small living room, Maddie told Erick that Heidi had driven away with a guy in a black car and that Matt thinks she's having an on going relationship but wants to keep it secret.

"Maddie, as long as she is not missing work hours or taking longer lunch times then she can do it and there is nothing we can do."

"But Erick, do you think it would be appropriate for me to ask her about it under the guise of concern for her."

"You can do anything you want since you are the owner and hired her. In fact, it might be interesting to see how she reacts when she knows that we know she is having some sort of a relationship with someone who she wants to keep secret."

"That's true, Erick, because if you think about it, when someone applies for a job here, we have questions on the application about their families such as spouses, children and other relationships, so I guess I'll talk to her."

"Erick, are you going back to the construction site today? I am going to do my regular check of the maids and checking the halls, rooms and bathrooms just to make sure all is shining and clean. Tomorrow I am going to The National Bank in Munising since a second appraiser is meeting me there."

"Well, have fun, honey, and I'll see you tonight. Erick bent over and kissed her goodbye. Maddie was startled by the kiss, and he actually called her 'honey.' Erick looked at her and asked if she were okay.

"I've never been better, honey." Then she pulled him close and kissed him goodbye too.

CHAPTER 37

Around 12:30 pm Maddie pulled into the parking lot of The National Bank. She had planned to arrive early to talk to a banker and set up a room to meet with Tom Holder, the appraiser.

Katie, one of the senior bankers led her to the safety deposit vault, then took Maddie's key and with her own key opened the door to the vault, then with Maddie's key opened the cubby where her safe deposit box was securely stored. She then led her to a brightly lighted room with a table and chairs where she had enough room to lay the painting on the table.

"Ms. Kirkpatrick, why don't you leave the painting in its box and come with me to the lobby where you can meet your appraiser. I'll lock this room. I'm the only one who has this key.

When the appraiser arrives, I will escort both of you back here. In fact, if you feel nervous about this I will show you where you can sit in the lobby which will give you a sightline back to the door of this room and at the same time you can keep an eye on the front door so you can see when the appraiser arrives."

Maddie sat in a comfortable modern style upholstered chair. Tom Holder arrived a few minutes ahead of 2pm when they were supposed to meet. Even though they had never met, she knew he must be the appraiser. Unlike most of the people coming into the bank in casual clothing, Tom Holder was dressed in a good looking black business suit with a white shirt and expensive looking tie and carrying a briefcase. Maddie figured his case held his appraiser tools. Maddie stood up and waved to him.

"You must be Ms. Kirkpatrick."

Extending her hand to his, she replied, "I am, and you must be Tom Holder."

"Yes, very nice to meet you but please call me Tom."

"And most people call me Maddie."

Maddie glanced over at Katie who had noticed that Tom and Maddie met, so she went over and introduced herself to Tom then led them back to the room.

"For your safety I am going to lock you into this room, but if you need anything or when you are ready to leave please push that red button on the wall. It has a buzzer on it and will buzz in my office so I will come back for any questions or to escort you to the vault when you leave."

After Katie left, Maddie gently removed the painting from the box and carefully laid it on the table. Tom opened his case and took out a special ultraviolet light and magnifying glass. As Nick had done, Tom put on a jeweler's head mounted visor with a small light on the front.

After an initial inspection, Tom Holder looked up and then explained, "This is a very old painting. I'm sure your first appraiser told you this since its frame tell tells us that. It appears that at one time it had an overpainting which was skillfully removed."

Maddie quickly replied, "Yes, Nick, the first appraiser at the Art Institute in Minneapolis removed the overpainting just a few days ago.

"Maddie, Nick is a wonderful conservator. I am not a conservator but can see the same characteristics that Nick saw so know how they can affect the value of a painting."

As the hours passed, Tom recounted many of the qualities Nick had mentioned. The painting was old, probably from the nineteenth century and probably from the Netherlands. It also was in good condition for its age since there was not much fading due to how and where it had been stored especially away from extreme weather conditions.

Tom did turn the painting over several times and saw the faint signature. With his magnifying glass and different lights he saw a part of a name which looked like 'Vander.' He couldn't make out the rest of the name. Tom explained to Maddie that Vander was the beginning of a surname or family name and meant 'of' or 'at the' or 'of the.'

"I will try to figure out the whole name. I have a stronger light in my car and a special kind of solvent that might make the rest of the name clear. You wait here Maddie and I'll be right back."

Tom buzzed Katie who opened the door within a couple minutes.

As Maddie waited, she looked closely at the painting. She had never taken an art course but prided herself in her decorating ability. The art background of the painting was interesting and she could see how art history combined with the artist's creativity in allowing colors to mix and flow including areas of light against the background gave the painting life as if it were real. She began to think that she wanted to showcase the painting for her guests to see, so would definitely look into purchasing one of the secure display cases that Dan Ford had recommended.

After a few minutes, but what seemed an eternity, Tom returned with another bag of appraiser tools.

Katie let him in and informed them that they had about an hour left before the bank would close.

Tom immediately went to work on the signature. The solvent had a strong odor. Tom had also brought in a stronger light for his camera. He aimed the light at the spot where he had seen the signature. The first part of the name 'Vander' became more clear as the solvent was applied. Then he applied the solvent next to 'Vander' and waited to see if the rest of the name would be revealed as the solvent soaked in and the light was directed very close to the signature. Within a few minutes the end of the name came into view just enough so Tom could see it. He took a picture of the whole signature which was Van der Berg. Tom knew the signature would be clear on the camera. He then took pictures of the painting from all different angles moving the light around as he moved to each new angle. He finally turned the painting over and took pictures of the back of the frame.

"Okay, Maddie, I have a fairly good idea of the name which is Van der Berg. The painter was definitely a Dutch painter."

He then reached in his case to retrieve a source book for Dutch names in order to find the definition of the name. He informed Maddie that Van der Berg meant 'from the cliff or mountain.'

"This really is a coincidence, Tom, since the lighthouse I bought is situated at the top of a cliff overlooking Lake Superior."

"Well, Maddie, now that I have all this information I won't be able to give you an appraisal for a few days since I have to go back to the office and analyze the results so I think we should leave now as the bank will be closing soon."

Maddie buzzed Katie after carefully packing the painting in its box. Katie then led them back to the vault where they safely locked it in its drawer then secured the door to the vault. They all exchanged cards with their contact numbers then went their separate ways. Maddie decided to drive the one hour back to the Twin Sisters Inn. She had more research to do but felt as though she was getting closer to the real story behind the painting.

A phone message was waiting for Maddie when she arrived at the inn. It was from Dan Ford of the Federal Bureau of Investigation. He informed her he was renting a furnished apartment near Sault Ste Marie which he was also going to use as his office. Dan left his contact information including his new address on Maple Ave.

CHAPTER 38

Maddie was glad to be back at the inn for a few days or at least until she received a phone call from Carolyn Hall, which came unexpectedly the day after Maddie returned to the inn.

Carolyn had talked to her husband, Doug, and they wanted to meet Maddie at the construction site since she and Doug wanted to visit their son, Wilson and to include him in the discussion. They were going to fly from Duluth to the closest airport then rent a car and drive to the ShipWreck Coast.

After breakfast, Maddie phoned Carolyn Hall to suggest a meeting place near the lighthouse.

"During your visit, Carolyn, we could meet at my hotel or yours whichever is convenient. Another idea is that I can ask my friend and neighbor, Glenn, who owns a beautiful hunting lodge behind the lighthouse if could we meet in his living room. He has been such a help to me and always keeps me up to date on what's going on at the construction site."

Carolyn said that would be fine and was looking forward to meeting her. When Maddie asked permission to include Erick as he knew all about the strange and dangerous situations that had been happening. Carolyn also agreed to that. They decided to meet at the lighthouse after lunch around 1pm and then if Glenn permitted, they would go back to his lodge.

Maddie immediately phoned Glenn to ask him about the group meeting at his lodge. He was delighted and excited to host them.

"But, Maddie, you should tell them about Toby in case anyone has allergies to dogs."

Maddie complied and found out that no one in the group had allergies.

The next morning the atmosphere was charged with excitement and huge expectations as Maddie planned to return to the ShipWreck Coast. She didn't want to seem impatient since the Halls needed time for a quiet visit with their son, Wil. She drove slowly to Munising. Erick was already at the site. Her mind swirled with all sorts of ideas and imaginings of what she would discover from the Hall's information. Although she had eaten breakfast at the inn, there was no time for lunch and she didn't care since she had no appetite due to the nervousness that had enveloped her.

Arriving at the construction site, she pulled into the front parking lot and noticed a strange car, probably the Hall's since they had arrived from Duluth that morning. Before leaving her car, she called Erick.

"Hi, honey, have the Hall's arrived yet?"

"Yes, they have and are very nice people. I think you'll enjoy them and all the information they'll have for you. They are in the lighthouse now where Wil is showing them around, so why don't you come over to the the keeper's house with me. I am starting to inspect then work on the fireplace. I will let them know you arrived and are with me."

"I'll be over as soon as I let Glenn know that I am here."

She walked over the luscious green lawn that led to the lodge. Glenn with Toby answered the door. Toby knew Maddie and wiggled an exciting welcome to her. Glenn was happy to see her and had everything set in place for their meeting.

"I'll see you in a few minutes, Glenn, as soon as the Hall's are finished with their tour of the lighthouse and thanks again for your hospitality."

When Maddie arrived at the keeper's house she found Erick inspecting the fireplace. He had a quizzical expression on his face. Greeting Maddie with a hug, he then backed off.

"I guess I better keep my mind on this inspection although that is hard to do that when my special love is here."

"Yeah, I feel the same way." Maddie blushed. "So, have you found anything suspicious?"

"I've just started but there is something different or strange about the brick walls encircling the inside of the fireplace."

"Well, I guess there is not much we can do as I see the Halls with Wil heading towards the keeper's house. I think this is going to be a long meeting."

Carolyn Hall was an attractive brunette in her late forties dressed in casual beige slacks wearing a cashmere indigo sweater and matching jacket. Her husband, Doug, was tall at just over six feet. He was dressed in jeans, sweater and an all weather jacket.

After introductions, the group crossed the lawn to Glenn's lodge. As usual, Glenn offered his guests an array of drinks and small snacks as they settled onto his couch and chairs around the fireplace.

Carolyn suggested that Maddie start with some of the questions concerning the painting.

Maddie began by sharing the information that Nick Johnson, the conservator at the Minneapolis Art Institute had discovered and also the thoughts of the second appraiser.

"I understand from Wil, Carolyn, that you had a relative named Joey who died in the battle of Holland during World War II and that he is a real hero in your family."

"Yes, Maddie, Joey was very special. I didn't know him since I was born years after World War II, but my parents and grandparents talked about him. You see right before he died he gave a letter to one of his commanders and was insistent that the letter be mailed immediately as it had important information for his relatives back here in or near the Shipwreck Coast.

Supposedly, it had something to do with another relative who lived in Holland and mailed a box to our relatives here in the United Sates. It contained a gift of great financial value that they needed to get out of Holland before the Nazis invaded the country. When the Nazis invaded a country, they would ransack people's homes and steal their valuables. The Holland relatives weren't sure they would be successful in fleeing Holland to the United States before being caught by the Nazis and either killed or sent to the camps. They were from my side of the family and were Jewish."

Doug then took over the conversation which included a time line of Hitler's rise to power. He described that how in 1933 when Hitler became Germany's Chancellor, he immediately began instituting policies that isolated the Jewish people and subjected them to persecution. These policies were meant to dehumanize the Jewish people. He described a policy in 1938 requiring Jews bearing the first names of non Jewish origin to adopt an additional name. For men, the name was "Israel" and for women, the name was "Sara." These names had to be added to their given names and they were required to carry identity cards that indicated their heritage. Finally, in 1938 all Jewish passports were stamped with an identifying red letter, 'J.'

Maddie looked at Carolyn as Doug was recounting the history and noticed her eyes filling with tears.

Wiping her eyes, Carolyn continued, "And all of this started early in 1933. The writings of known German writers were burned in a communal ceremony at Berlin's Opera House and German businesses would no longer support Jewish businesses and Jews couldn't become full German citizens."

"But Carolyn," Maddie asked, "Weren't your relatives from Holland?"

"Yes, Maddie, but although Holland attempted to remain neutral, and at first, Hitler promised they could stay neutral, German forces invaded the country in May, 1940 beginning five years of occupation."

Wil broke his silence, "But Mom, why don't you tell them what happened in 1938. It was the incident of "Kristallnacht.' That would relate to the paintings, art and other valuables.

"Okay, Wilson, you're right. We're really here to find out about Maddie's painting. Kristallnacht is known in English as the 'Night of Broken Glass.' It happened over two nights on November 9th and November 10th, 1938. These were nights of terror. Nazis in Germany and Holland torched synagogues, hospitals, vandalized Jewish homes, schools, and businesses and murdered close to one hundred Jews. Most of the Jews were very successful business men and also government workers. They had many valuables such as paintings, jewelry and gems among other things.

Wil again stepped into the conversation, "And Maddie, that's why many Jews who expected something as horrible as those two nights took their valuable paintings and overpainted them to make them look as if they had little value. Then, they tried to get them out of their home and send them overseas for friends or relatives to keep them safe until they could escape and leave their country.

And, that's where Joey came in. Our relatives in Holland were very shrewd and had mailed their paintings and other valuables out of Europe., but they had to let our American relatives know that these valuables were on the way to them in America. Some how they had gotten in touch with Joey as he was fighting the war in Holland and sent a letter to him with information about the valuables and to alert the American relatives for their arrival. After the valuables were successfully mailed, our Dutch relatives tried to flee."

Maddie asked, "Did your Holland relatives make it to the United States?"

Wil glanced at his mom,.

"You explain that one Mom."

"After our American relatives received the letter, they never heard from the Holland relatives. Sadly, we don't know what happened. I think they made it out of Holland. We heard that the best country to escape to was Portugal as it was neutral and friendly with the Allies.

Portugal allowed many thousands of Jews to reach the port of Lisbon so a number of American and French organizations helped the refugees in Lisbon to reach the United States."

Then Carolyn explained that in those days even if they had booked passage on a freighter, when the ships arrived at the United States ports, many of the ports would not allow a lot of the Jewish people to disembark. In Europe it was also like that because countries like ours had quotas on how many Jewish people could enter the country. What was also difficult was that Germany and other Nazi held countries absconded with half their income before allowing the people to leave, thus many Jews arrived in other countries with very little money.

Wil chimed in again, "We need to talk about what's happened to all the valuables the Nazis looted from the Jewish people. In my studies I have learned that in the last seventy five years or so these looted valuables have passed through many hands and down through generations. There is also the subject of the museums which have these looted paintings hanging on their walls and don't even know it. I've also heard there are groups of people who surreptitiously try to find the looted paintings and offer to buy them from people who don't even know they are in the possession of a valuable painting so the owner will sell it for a very undervalued price.

Maddie added, "Yes, Wil, I've started realizing that, and also am learning that these groups will go to no lengths to get their hands on these valuable items."

"Yeah", Erick spoke up, "like the poisonous Pasty?" "I still think there's danger in the air around here."

Carolyn looked shocked.

"I'm not sure I want my son working here if it's not safe."

"Mom, I am safe here. I have all the guys working around me."

Erick immediately spoke up, "Don't worry, Carolyn, we're all looking after Wil."

Maddie didn't feel that threatened since she knew Dan Ford from the FBI was investigating this and was close by, but decided not to say anything.

As the conversation ended, the Halls decided to check out some of the local restaurants in the local area, then spend the night with Wil before flying back to Duluth. Everyone promised to inform each other if new information came to light. Erick and Maddie decided to return to the Twin Sisters Inn in Sault Ste. Marie the next day. Maddie hoped for a call from Dan Ford concerning his investigation.

Chapter 39

Dan Ford had wasted no time to quickly settle in to his temporary home and office in Sioux Ste. Marie. He knew Maddie's life was in danger even if she had secured a safe place for the painting so was glad she wasn't in town while he began his investigation.

Dan had been trained by the FBI's 'Rapid Deployment Team.' The specialized training included training in art and cultural property. The training also consisted of assisting in investigations world wide in cooperation with foreign law enforcement officials. The FBI had legal attache offices. Their art crime team was provided special trial attorneys by the US Department of Justice for prosecutorial support.

Dan began making contact with all the museums around the Sault Ste. Marie cities—the one in Michigan, USA, and the one across the International Bridge in Ontario, Canada. The Canadian Sault Ste. Marie was a larger city and had most of the museums. The museums contained artifacts and cultural history of the area including the Native Indian history. Some had paintings. Dan met the curators checking to see if they had a history of art theft.

Most had experienced theft at one time or another, mostly of cultural artifacts of some of which could be equally as valuable as paintings.

During his questioning of the curators, he very carefully tried to discover if they knew of any art theft rings operating in the area. He knew it was a delicate matter as in some museums there were staff who could have been placed there by the art theft groups. Most curators said they had heard of them, but had seen no evidence of any in the area.

Dan asked if their museums had had a theft did they catch the thief and, if so, was it traced back to an organization or was it just a single lone thief.

In one case there was a single thief and he was caught and was serving time. In another case there was evidence of three thieves, however, they had not been caught and the case is presently a cold case. Unfortunately, they had gotten away with two very valuable native artifacts.

The FBI had checked some of the crafty ways thieves try to gain off the artifacts such as to hold the work for ransom from the museum, or from art insurance companies. They would even try to sell the artifacts on the black market where drug traffickers use stolen art work by trading it for weapons. Sometimes the artifacts end up in the hands of mobsters who use them in exchange for reduced prison sentences. However, the worst fear for the authorities is if the thieves can't find a way to get money for the artifacts without being caught, they will throw them away or destroy them.

Dan Ford also considered the border between Canada and the United States. All of the main cities in Canada were across the border from major US cities with bridges and customs connecting them. In Canada most of the people lived within one hundred miles of the border as most of the country is uninhabitable due to the very cold weather.

With all of this, it still would be difficult for art thieves to drive their stolen goods across the bridges into the USA because of the customs and border control. Even if robbers had access to a private plane, there was still the problem of sneaking the artifacts through customs unless some of the groups were hooked up with larger influential groups such as a cartel who could place some of their members into the customs jobs.

Dan made a mental note to ask his Art Crime Team if they have evidence of international cartels being involved in stolen art and, if so, where have they been operating. He wouldn't be surprised if there was the branch of a cartel in the area.

As Dan left Canada and crossed back into the United States, his next step would be to visit Maddie's Twin Sisters Inn. When he walked through the front door of the inn, he saw Matt and Heidi at the front desk and asked if Madeline Kirkpatrick were there. As he asked the question, he held up his FBI identification.

Matt answered, "Oh, you're with the FBI? Ms. Kirkpatrick is out of town but will return sometime tomorrow. Is anything wrong?"

Dan noticed a look of fear come over Heidi's face.

"No, nothing is wrong. Ms. Kirkpatrick and I just have some business to discuss so I'll check back tomorrow. The FBI has just opened a satellite office in Sioux Ste. Marie, and this is where she can reach me. Here is my card. I would appreciate it if you would give it to her. Thanks again."

As soon as Dan Ford walked out the door, Matt and Heidi looked at each other. Heidi's eyes were wide with fear.

"What's wrong Heidi? He's just an FBI agent. Perhaps crime has risen in the area and he wants to help. After all, why would the FBI open an office in this small town?"

Heidi excused herself as she needed a restroom break. Since no one was in the restroom, she pulled out her I Phone and placed a call. Before hanging up, she responded, "Okay, hope to see you in an hour. Will be looking for you."

After she had taken her place at the front desk, Heidi asked Matt if she could go to lunch in an hour. Looking the other way and rolling his eyes Matt replied, "Fine, do what you want, Heidi. But no more than an hour since I'll be starving by then."

With a sly smile on her face and sarcasm in her voice, Heidi assured him she would be on time.

As soon as a black car drove up in front of the inn, Heidi slung her purse over her shoulder and headed for the car door. Unbeknown to Heidi, Dan Ford had taken a seat in a cafe across the street that had an outdoor area which was glassed in due to the cold weather. He had a camera with a telescopic lens and immediately left the cafe and positioned himself behind the car but on the other side of the street. Before the car pulled away he was able to snap a picture of the license plate. He then returned to the cafe and ordered a steak for lunch while keeping an eye on the front door of the inn. He decided to wait there until the car returned knowing that Heidi would probably have no more then an hour for lunch. He finished his lunch before the hour was up so ordered a cup of coffee and asked for the bill. Dan also phoned the FBI and gave them the license plate number to check immediately and also to check the background of the owner of the car. He then asked to be transferred to the Art Crime Team where he asked for information on the possibility of art theft teams being backed by a cartel and, if so, where were they operating. He wanted this information for his meeting with Maddie when she returned.

He then paid for his meal with cash left on the table tucked into the black bill book so he could leave immediately if necessary.

He didn't have to wait long. The black car pulled up in front of the inn. The windows were tinted so he couldn't see who was driving. Heidi got out and seemed to linger while talking to the driver. Dan had a chance to take a photo of her as she stood at the car door. She then closed the car door and entered the inn.

Dan immediately left the cafe to watch where the car would go. The car made a U-turn and surprisingly turned into the side street which was next to the building across the street from the inn. Dan jogged as fast as he could to see where on the side street the car was going. It was hard to believe but the car turned into the parking lot which belonged to the building across from the inn. When the driver got out, Dan snapped a few quick shots with his camera. He did not get a full face picture but a full side picture with his profile. Dan planned on sending the photos to the FBI.

There was a back door to the building and Dan positioned himself near the door. He knew that the man had never seen him so as the man unlocked the door, Dan moved to behind the man and when the door opened, Dan yelled, "Hey can you hold door for me. I have to get to my client."

The man held the door and Dan followed him to the elevator after thanking him. He saw the man press the button for the fifth floor. Dan pushed the bottom for the seventh floor. When the man left the elevator at the fifth floor, Dan held the door open until he saw the man take a right turn down the hall. Dan stepped out of the elevator and let the door close. Silently he went right and with his camera without the flash saw the man stop at the door on the side of the hallway facing the main street. His room looked out on main street and was directly in front of the inn.

Quickly leaving the building, Dan walked back to the main street after taking photos of the black car from all angles. He immediately sent all the pictures to the Art Crime Unit so they could have a picture of Heidi and the man.

Sauntering down main street Dan found the shops friendly and charming. Not many shoppers were in the stores since it was a working day in the middle of the afternoon.

When he told the store owners, he was from the FBI and had opened a small office on Maple Ave., they were curious and overjoyed to have an FBI presence in their little town. He urged them to call him any time if they needed any type of criminal investigation, but first and foremost not to forget the assistance of their town's police force.

Dan also walked through the beautiful park run by Homeland Security to watch how the locks worked. He was glad they had security around the locks since so many of the freighters coming through were from all over the world. It was also a main place where crew members could embark and disembark. At the security point located at the entrance to the park, crew members and visitors had to go through a security check and especially crew members had to show proof and ID before boarding a freighter.

Even with all the security, Dan wondered how many incidents of smuggling took place. No system is one hundred per cent secure.

Since it was late afternoon, Dan decided to head back to his apartment and office to call Maddie in order to find out when she would return to Sault Ste. Marie. Hopefully, it would be by the evening or the next morning.

Chapter 40

Erick and Maddie arrived at the Inn around ten in the morning after spending a couple nights at Glenn's house. Erick had to finish some work at the lighthouse. They had driven their own cars back.

"I promised Brad I'd be back tomorrow to work on the fireplace in the keeper's house. Are you going to stay in Sault Ste. Marie?"

"Yes, I promised Matt I would stay a while until I can get some results from Dan Ford's investigation. I feel safer here and I have bills to pay and other paper work regarding the inn which I need to complete. It is the time of the month when I have to reorder many products."

Matt breathed a sigh of relief when he saw Maddie and Erick walk through the front doorway. Matt signaled to Maddie that he needed to talk in private. She waved for him to follow her and Erick to her apartment.

"Maddie, an FBI agent named Dan Ford came in and was asking for you. What's going on? Heidi seemed to be very uncomfortable that he was here. I told her there was nothing to be afraid of."

"Don't worry, Matt. He is helping me investigate some of the weird things which have been happening out at the lighthouse. He thinks my life is in danger."

"Wow, that's scary. I'll be on the look out for anything that seems strange at the Inn but I'm not going to tell Heidi because she may freak out."

"I think that is best too, Matt. Only you and I and Erick know about this. I don't even want the Sheriff in Munising to know since he may have a conflict as of our working with the FBI."

"I have one phone message for you, Maddie. A Tom Holder called you and wants you to call back."

After Matt returned to the front desk, Maddie phoned Tom Holder.

"I'm glad you called back so soon, Maddie. I have what I think is a fairly accurate appraisal of your painting. I'm glad your painting is safe in the bank since it is quite valuable. Nick Johnson's appraisal is quite close to mine. I, too, think it is worth around a half a million dollars to just under two million, give or take either way."

Maddie's heart began to race. She was excited, but also felt vulnerable because of its value.

She would ask Dan Ford to recommend the safest and most secure display cabinet which he had mentioned when they were at the Art Institute in Minneapolis. She wondered if she ever would feel safe with the painting hanging in the inn, but at least it was safe for now. She had just hung up from Tom's call when the phone rang again. It was Dan Ford.

"I have a lot to show you, Ms. Kirkpatrick, and I think you and I should meet immediately. I think the best place would be at my apartment on Maple Avenue. Can you drive over here right away? I would also like your friend, Erick, to hear this if that's okay with you."

Maddie agreed and was glad Erick had decided to stay for the day. They left to meet Dan Ford and were looking forward excitedly to hear what he had seen.

Maddie was surprised at how attractive and professional his apartment appeared. After all, it was his office too. It was furnished with a red leather couch and two red leather chairs facing each other with an octagonal table in between. He suggested they stay in the living room since his office was rather small. He offered them coffee or tea which they gratefully accepted. When he left to retrieve a tray of snacks from the kitchen, Maddie leaned over to Erick, "I think he wants us to be relaxed and feel comfortable around him so we will feel it's okay to open up about all we know."

After setting the tray of snacks on the coffee table, he began his story, "I began checking out the museums in Sault Ste. Marie, Canada and talked to the curators to get a sense if they knew of any art thefts here as there were in Minneapolis. They told me there had been a few. In one case a thief was caught but in another the thieves were never caught. Two valuable native artifacts had been stolen. I'm not sure if there is an art theft ring around here unless they belong to a cartel who could sneak the stolen goods across the Canadian border and past customs. That would be very tricky but some of the cartels are very sophisticated in trafficking stolen goods.

Then, I walked around your fair city and talked to the merchants to get a feel of how safe they feel around here and if they have ever been robbed. They seemed to be excited to have an FBI agent living close by, but I also got the feeling that this is a peaceful town and fairly safe."

Dan Ford then explained that he always carries a camera with a telescopic lens and there were many times when he used it on his walk around.

"Now here comes the interesting part. I visited your inn and asked for you even though I knew you hadn't returned. I talked to Matt who was very cooperative, but when I showed my FBI badge, it didn't bother Matt at all, but I could see the girl working at the counter was very worried and seemed scared.

When I left the inn, I went across the street to the café with the glassed in outdoor seating area. I hadn't been there long when a black car pulled up in front of your inn and the girl from the front desk came out and got in the car. The windows were tinted. I couldn't see a driver, but I was able to get outside in time to take a picture of the license plate as the car pulled away. After that, I decided to hang around the café for lunch since I figured she'd have to return after her lunch break. I timed it and she took an hour. When she got out of the car, she lingered at the door talking to the driver. I also took a picture of that. When the car left, it made a U-turn. By that time I was outside. I saw the car turn down the street next to the building directly across the street from your inn. That surprised me. I ran to the back of that building and saw the car turn into the parking lot that belonged to the building. I saw the man get out and was able to take a picture of him walking to the back door. I rushed over as he was opening the door and he held it open for me. We both went up the elevator. He got off on the fifth floor. Although I had pushed the button for the seventh floor, when he got off and turned to go down the hall, I kept the door open and took a picture of him at his door. He is on the side of the hotel which looks directly out and onto main street and your inn. I have sent copies of these pictures to the FBI and am waiting for information on both the girl and the guy."

Dan then showed them the pictures. When Erick saw the one of the man, he was sure that even though it was a side or profile picture of him walking across the parking lot and also the picture at his hotel door, it looked very much like the man who was in the restaurant with Heidi in Canada.

"So, I guess we are being spied on", Maddie responded.

"Well, Ms. Kirkpatrick, you're right, but I am going to get a warrant to search his room."

Before he could continue the conversation, Dan's phone rang.

"Great timing, it's the FBI lab. Excuse me for a minute."

Dan Ford returned with a look of success.

"Okay, we traced the license, and the car belongs to a Mark Bronson. We also have some information on his background. He is a former art dealer, but here's the rub, there have been many times when he has been a suspect in nefarious art dealings, however, there was never enough proof to accuse him of anything. He is not an art dealer now, but when he was, he traveled extensively in Europe, South America and throughout the United States. Because of the strange happenings around your lighthouse, Ms. Kirkpatrick, I am putting him on the FBI watch list. I am getting a search warrant for his room tomorrow and will report to you what I find. In the meantime you should be vigilant and please report to me any other occurrences you might experience. Hopefully, I will have more information for you after I search his room",

Getting up to leave, Maddie and Erick thanked him, and told Dan they could see some connections taking place and would look forward to his call, hopefully, the next day.

On the way home Erick reminded Maddie that he had to go back to the lighthouse in the morning and she should phone him if Dan finds anything strange after he searches Mark Bronson's room.

Chapter 41

Dan Ford woke up early. The FBI had faxed a search warrant to him. He knew he'd have to wait until Mark Bronson left his room. In the meantime he looked up the building and room designs to give him an idea of how long the search would be.

The building where Bronson lived had rooms more like efficiency apartments with one bedroom and a separate sitting area with a television and small kitchen. The kitchen had a refrigerator, microwave, regular oven and a four burner stove. The information also showed that the shelves were fully stocked with bowls, glasses, silverware, cooking utensils, and pots and pans. Most of the mainline hotel chains had a similar set up with a bedroom, and a sitting room outside of the bedroom area with couches, tables and a kitchen counter, a stove and oven. The sitting room was called a suite. This hotel was a cheaper brand then the mainline hotels.

Special Agent Ford then called the FBI back to see if they had information on Mark Bronson's present career which might give him an idea of his working hours. It only took a few minutes before they called him back. Their findings indicated that he was in pharmaceutical sales which meant that he would have regular hours but would be on the road most of the day.

Around ten o'clock in the morning Dan Ford drove to Mark Bronson's building. He parked behind it in the guest parking lot. He walked around the parking lot and did not see the black car with the license number the FBI had sent to him which was the same as Dan had taken a picture of. Dan surmised that he must be on the road selling pharmaceuticals. He then walked around to the front door assuming it would be open since that would be where the front desk is for those checking in to the hotel.

He approached the front desk where the desk clerk was just finishing a phone call. After hanging up, she asked how she could help.

"I'm Special Agent Ford with the FBI", Dan said while holding up his badge.

"I have a warrant here to search the fifth floor room that belongs to Mark Bronson."

He showed the warrant to the clerk. The clerk said she would take him to the manager's office behind the front desk. Dan showed him the warrant and proof of Bronson's driver's license. The manager whose name was Jim told Dan he would have to escort him to the room and would stay in the room while Dan looked around.

"Mr. Bronson is at work and will not be back until this evening but that doesn't make any difference as long as I am with you in the room while you are doing what you have to do."

As they approached Bronson's room, #521, Ford scanned the hallway. There was no activity. Most guests had probably checked out.

Entering the room, they switched on the hall light. The curtains were closed giving the suite a feeling that it was still nighttime. They walked through the sitting area which had a couch, coffee table and a couple of chairs across from the kitchen counter, a refrigerator, stove and oven plus microwave. Somehow they had been able to fit a large screen television on the side of the wall next to an archway that led to the bedroom where there was a king sized bed, chairs, closet and chest of drawers with a mirror above the chest.

Dan quickly opened the curtains. The sunlight streamed into the room changing the whole feeling of the atmosphere. On a desk next to the chest of drawers, Dan saw some small items, but first turned to what was standing in front of the window—a very expensive looking telescope on a tripod that was aimed directly at the window overlooking the Twin Sisters Inn.

Having researched all sorts of spy gadgets during his time at the FBI including telescopes and periscopes, he could tell that the telescope was one of the 4K Super Telephoto Zoom Monocular telescopes that could bring you closer to objects then ever before. It's purpose was to achieve maximum magnification at the smallest effective aperture.

Jim whistled, then commented.

"That's one beautiful telescope. It must cost a fortune."

"It does. The resolution angle is forty seven times that of ordinary telescopes. I believe its the first to achieve great magnification and clarity on such a small scale, thus capturing amazingly sharp photos."

"Why would Mr. Bronson have something like this here?" Jim asked.

Dan explained that if he were a hunter, he could capture great images of wild life from a long distance away.

"But I don't think that this is his mission here. I'm sure he has been spying on the Twin Sisters Inn."

"Why would he do that, Agent Ford?"

"That is what we are trying to find out. The telescope also has a built in night function. If there are no terrain obstacles you can easily observe people or things six miles away. This means he can probably look into those rooms directly across the street at the inn."

Dan Ford then turned to the desk to check out the gadgets laying on top. He saw an alarm clock that didn't belong to the hotel. There was a desk calculator, and a couple of pens.

There were also two GPS trackers that could be attached to cars or other items so they could be tracked and located at all times. Dan thought of the maroon rental car and Mr. Bronson's black car and how they had been followed, according to Maddie, all the way to Minneapolis.

Dan turned to Jim and pointed out some of the items on the table.

"What we have here is a stash of spy equipment. Take a look at the alarm clock. It probably has a hidden camera in it including a DVR recording or other secret recording method. It may have motion activation which would record only when there is movement in the room. See the keychain behind the clock. It probably has an audio recorder. The same goes for pens and watches. These clever disguises make audio recording easy. There is probably a memory card in each that you can take out and put in your computer."

Dan then suggested that they don't touch anything so their fingerprints wouldn't smear the prints which are already on the items.

Dan did have gloves on but he didn't want anything moved that he had taken pictures of such as the telescope and the array of gadgets, then suggested they close the drapes and leave the room just as they found it.

"I would prefer that you don't tell Mr. Bronson we were in his room."

Jim said he would keep the secret and ask his employee at the front desk not to say anything to Mr. Bronson.

"I don't know how kosher keeping the secret is, but around here we do pretty much as we want."

Dan Ford thanked Jim, then left to find Maddie. Matt was the only one at the front desk as Dan entered the inn. Heidi had taken an early lunch break.

"Ms. Kirkpatrick is in her apartment. I'll let her know you're on your way back."

Dan tapped on her door. She opened it immediately anticipating good news.

Dan began by saying he had learned a lot about Mark Bronson explaining his background as a former art dealer, but now was a pharmaceutical sales man in this area.

"Do you think, Agent Ford, he could have been the one who put the arsenic in my Pasty sandwich?"

"He might as well be, Ms Kirkpatrick. He seems to be quite shrewd and knows a lot about spy equipment. Also, since he is a pharmaceutical sales rep. he probably has access to drugs and poisons too."

Maddie was disturbed to learn about the telescope he had which was pointed at the inn and also the little spy gadgets he had.

"Do you think he is just using the spy equipment in his apartment or could he have bugged my inn too?"

Agent Ford didn't think so since Bronson had never been in the inn. But if she wanted him to look around the inn, he would, however, thought they should wait. Agent Ford did not want to arouse suspicions. He also told Maddie that Jim, the apartment/hotel manager across the street was not going to tell Bronson that they had been in his room.

As soon as Agent Ford had left, the phone rang and it was Erick.

"Maddie, it's been a crazy day at the lighthouse. I didn't want to bother you since I knew you were waiting for information from Agent

Ford, but when I arrived at the keeper's house, I found the inside in shambles. Someone was in here last night and made a mess of it. Again, it's as if they were looking for something. I checked with Glenn and he said Toby was barking on and off as if he knew a stranger was around. Glenn also said he saw a flashlight as someone walked from room to room. I've checked with the workers and they didn't know anything about it. They all have keys to the lighthouse and keeper's house, but I don't think they are involved.

"Remember, Erick, we had the locks changed. Who else might have gotten or stolen a key? And also remember that the painting is locked in the bank. Whoever broke in might not have known that or there is something else they know that we don't so the danger still continues."

"I don't have any answers yet, Maddie, but I spent the morning cleaning up around the keeper's house then will start refurbishing the fireplace."

Maddie told Erick about Agent Ford's findings.

"I still can't put two and two together on this mystery, but think we are getting closer."

When Erick arrived back at the inn for dinner and the night, Maddie asked him how much progress he had made on the downstairs bedrooms of the keeper's house.

"Well, I've cleared them of debris. There are hardwood floors so after a good shine, we should buy an attractive area rug."

"I can do that, honey. How is the plumbing? I know we have a workable shower, toilet, and sink. So, Erick, if I can get someone to move a bed and some chest of drawers with lamps, would you be willing to sleep in the keeper's house a few nights a week so you can guard the place? Hopefully, if someone comes around, you might have a better idea of who it is. You also have a gun and if you need help, Glenn is just across the lawn in the lodge."

"So, the love of my life wants me in a dangerous situation, he teased."

"Of course not, Erick. You know how I feel. Here's another idea, maybe Glenn will let Toby stay with you over night. Toby seems to like you, and certainly would hear someone stalking around the house before you or I could hear anything.."

Erick came over to Maddie and took her in his arms.

"Maybe, one day both of us will live out here. Don't worry, I can handle it.."

Maddie's mind started planning how to decorate the bedroom located by the front door which looked towards Glenn's house. The next day she would go shopping for furniture. She wanted Erick to feel at home and comfortable in the keeper's house, although she would miss him so much not staying at the Twin Sisters Inn.

The next morning Erick left for the Shipwreck Coast, and Maddie used the day scouring furniture shops. She figured she would choose old fashioned furniture as close as possible to early twentieth century furniture. There were many furniture stores near Sault Ste. Marie.

She chose a king size bed for the front bedroom hoping it would not take up most of the room. Then, she bought a small chest of drawers, two bedside tables, mirror for above the chest of drawers, and a full length mirror for the wall next to the bathroom door and closet. She visited a carpet company and chose a beautiful pale blue wall to wall carpeting. Since this bedroom would be the first to be decorated, she had to choose the bathroom fixtures. She chose another light blue color for the bathroom walls then gold bathroom fixtures around the sink and tub and gold bars for hanging towels. In the bedroom, she chose nautical blue lampshades for both side tables.

As Maddie went through the decorating procedure, she began to feel that she should stay with Erick in the keeper's house. Although he could take care of himself, she really didn't want him to stay alone. She began to rationalize that if she stayed with him and as the work on the keeper's house and lighthouse continued, it would give her more decorating ideas which would come with living in the atmosphere on the Shipwreck Coast. The area surrounding the Shipwreck Coast was quite different from the town of Sault Ste. Marie. As she thought more about it, she realized that she felt this way because she really didn't want to be away from Erick. She knew she loved him. So, Maddie planned on talking to Erick when he returned to the inn in the evening.

As the late afternoon turned to evening shadows, a storm moved into Sault Ste. Marie. A slash of lightening streaked across the sky. The rumble of thunder sounded in the distance. Then, came the pelting rain as hard as a tropical storm. The early evening sky turned to pitch darkness. The lights in the inn blinked a few times. Heidi and Matt retrieved their flashlights from under the counter of the front desk. Both Matt and Heidi laid their flash lights on the counter then found three storm lanterns which, when turned on, gave a cozy light to the front room and desk.

Maddie was worried about Erick and tried to call him with no success. She figured he should be in his car driving from the Shipwreck Coast to Sault Ste. Marie. She found her special storm phone that was battery operated. Again, she called Erick, but he didn't answer. Her phone was attached to a battery operated radio so she turned to the local weather. The forecast was not good. Between the Shipwreck Coast and Sault Ste. Marie there were high winds, no visibility and pounding rain. Everyone was advised to take cover. Maddie tried to call Brad Elstad, the head of the construction group but there was no answer. Then, Maddie called Glenn Pedersen, and finally he answered.

"Glenn, what's your weather out there. It's horrible here."

"Maddie, it's pretty bad out here. We have hurricane force winds, so most of the construction crew have left. Toby and I are safe, and weirdly, our electricity is still on."

"Glenn, have you seen Erick?"

"No, I haven't. I thought he had left with the construction crew when they cleared out of here around 4pm. I've heard the road between here and Sault Ste. Marie is mostly under water. Most of the crew lives in that direction. But, Maddie, if I hear any updates about the crew I'll let you know. Also, why don't you check the hotel in Munising. Some of the construction people might have booked rooms there rather than taking a chance on the roads."

After hanging up, Maddie called the hotels in Munising. They had no residents under Erick's name or any of the construction crew.

The storm in Sault Ste. Marie was worsening. The wind gusts were over sixty miles per hour. Maddie tried calling Erick again on her cell phone. There was no answer, only the answering machine. Maddie sent her message to his machine, "Erick, where are you? The storm is bad here. Please call me. I love you, Maddie."

Maddie then checked with the front desk. She was also concerned about Matt and Heidi. Heidi had her room at the inn so she invited Matt to stay and he accepted. At least they would be safe and they would all be together. Maddie knew that the breakfast crew would be unable to come in the next morning, but they had enough food for themselves and anyone staying at or just taking cover at the inn.

Maddie heard a tree crack outside and prayed that it wouldn't land on the inn. She wouldn't know until the next day the condition of the inn. She expected some shingles to be gone, and possible broken glass and flooding. But all she really cared about was Erick's safety. At least he had a key to the inn if he returned before morning.

After closing the front desk, and making sure that Heidi and Matt were safe and comfortable in their rooms, she locked the front door, kept a battery operated lamp on, then using her flashlight to light the way, she retired to her apartment.

CHAPTER 42

The storm had hit the Shipwreck Coast first before reaching Sault Ste. Marie. Most of the country roads were flooded.

Erick had been so busy cleaning up and inspecting the fireplace that he was oblivious to the turn of the weather. The keeper's house darkened with the arrival of the storm. So involved with his work, he just thought that the time had passed so fast it must be sundown. Finally, when a gust of wind over sixty miles per hour shook the house followed by a tropical rain with hail as big as golf balls, his concentration was broken. He opened the door to face night like sky followed by a strong gust of wind hitting his face so hard that he almost fell over backwards. He grabbed a flashlight from a table by the door and holding onto the frame around the door, he tried to scan his flashlight around the yard to see what damage there was. He could see that Glenn's lights were out and that Glenn had lighted some hurricane lamps. The wind was so strong he decided he couldn't make it up to Glenn's lodge. There were limbs and sticks and some construction debris flying around like missiles through the air. One strike on Erick would render him unconscious.

Erick decided he had to stay the night. When the storm calmed down he would get his sleeping bag from the truck. That would also give him the opportunity to turn on his truck's lights to survey the damage. Hopefully, there might be some snacks in the truck.

Erick tried to phone Maddie but there was no signal. He couldn't even call Glenn to check on him.

"Oh well", he thought, "I'll rig my flashlight up around the fireplace so I can continue my assessment of what needs to be fixed."

The fireplace had a beautiful tile surround which matched the brick wall at the back of the fireplace. There was a raised hearth in front of it also made of brick. Inside the fireplace leaning against the walls were a pair of old wrought iron andirons with a fire basket that would sit on the rails of each andiron. All parts of the fireplace were old and needed cleaning and polishing but, for its age the fireplace was in good shape.

Erick wondered how long it had been since anyone had built a fire. Erick was also aware that when the fireplace was restored, he would have to have a fire inspector who would inspect the chimney as well as the fireplace. So, Erick would have to be as thorough as he could with his inspection and repairs if needed.

The wind had become stronger. Gusts were at least seventy or eighty miles an hour. The old house vibrated. As the wind whistled around the corners of the house, it sounded like the scream of a woman almost as if it were warning Erick about something. He wished he could just relax by watching a fire where flames would be like dancing tongues beckoning him into their reality. As the storm raged on outside Erick almost felt mesmerized by the whole atmosphere, but at this point he could do nothing. He just had to wait out the storm before his phone would work and he could contact Maddie.

CHAPTER 43

Mark Bronson opened the door to his efficiency apartment across from the Twin Sisters Inn. There was no clue that the FBI or anyone had been in his apartment. He immediately went to his spy equipment. The Twin Sisters Inn was totally dark as was his apartment.

He pointed the telescope towards the inn. He still could see inside the lobby area because of the lighted lanterns. The whole town was dark. This was the perfect time to complete the Second part of his mission. As he thought of it, his phone rang.

"Hello", he answered, then continued, "Yes, I understand. Now is the time we have to act. I know the roads to the Shipwreck Coast are underwater, but I think my truck will make it through. Every place from here to the Shipwreck Coast is in the dark. No one will expect us. We have to complete the discovery and the mission now before daylight and before the storm passes."

He listened to the person on the other end of the line.

"Don't worry, boss, the only guy who might be in our way is that guy, Erick, a friend of Ms. Kirkpatrick. I can deal with him, but will need time to figure out where the goods are in the keeper's house."

Bronson listened to his boss, then added, "I'll need your backup over there and will need you to send support. I can't do this alone."

His boss asked him some other questions and Bronson replied, "I know about the painting which is safe in the bank, but we can deal with that later. Now we have to find the rest of the stuff. Remember our group has been growing this mission since World War II or at least seventy six years and won't stop now."

Bronson checked his road map for directions, packed his weapons, took his rain coat and boots and the special keys that he had received from a secret source. The keys would unlock the doors to the keeper's house and to the lighthouse.

The storm had become their savior allowing them to continue and solve this part of their World War II mission as unpatriotic and corrupt as it was.

CHAPTER 44

Erick had given up on getting out of the Shipwreck Coast before daylight. He wanted to stay at the keeper's house to protect it if he could. The house had become colder with a damp feeling due to the storm outside. He wished he had some wood but was afraid to build a fire without having a chimney inspection. So, he decided to sleep in his truck. His seat in the truck reclined. He could lock the doors and pile some blankets around him. After locking the keeper's house, he headed for his truck. His body fought against the gusts of wind. Once in the truck, he turned on the engine and lights to warm up the heater. The lights revealed the damage in the area, not to the lighthouse or keeper's house, but to the trees and foliage. Construction debris was strewn between the keeper's house and the lighthouse including against the enclosed walkway that connected both buildings. He imagined the clean up the next day would be horrible and back breaking. It could set them back a few days. He hoped the crew would be able to make it back in the morning but doubted it. He, Glenn and Toby were the only ones there.

As the night wore on, he settled himself in the truck. Fortunately, he found more bottles of water in the back of the truck and an extra sandwich he had brought from the inn. He even turned on the radio switching from one station to another to find the local news or weather report, but to no avail. Most stations didn't come through and if they did, the sound was such a snowy sound or white noise that he could barely understand what was being reported.

Dozing off, he was unaware of the pickup trucks assembling at the fringe of the property. Their lights were turned off.

Erick finally fell into a deep sleep at the same time a group of shadowy figures stalked very quietly towards the keeper's house. Their flashlights were off. They saw Erick's truck. Their leader quietly looked inside and saw Erick fast asleep. He gave a signal to the group that Erick was not a threat so immediately went to the front door of the keeper's house. A few of them went to the lighthouse. They all had keys to both buildings. Their mission was to find the rest of the lost loot stolen from the Jewish people in World War II, then to keep it for themselves. They felt secure since they were part of a larger international group which had been in existence for years since World War II. They were also part of many subgroups around the world. No one could get in their way. The money they made was in the billions. If they exceeded, they were handsomely paid, so they could not stop at anything even murder.

Somehow, their organizations had led them to this part of the isolated Shipwreck Coast and to these two buildings believing there was a fortune awaiting them.

They successfully opened the doors to both the keeper's house and the lighthouse. Once in, they turned on their flashlights. Their mission was to check every corner including all closets, shelves and to look for secret hiding places. They pushed on the walls hoping they might move to reveal other rooms. They checked tiles in the bathroom and kitchen hoping to find some loose tiles which when removed might reveal doors to hidden cubby holes.

These groups were well trained and had been searching places for years and knew every trick, or at least that is what they thought. They had to operate quickly but carefully since, particularly in the case that both houses were under remodeling, it was difficult to negotiate around the construction debris.

Their cell phones were set to vibrate to alert them that someone was calling. It would be too dangerous to have a phone ring. Finally, the leader of the keeper's house group called the leader of the lighthouse group. No one had found anything yet. They decided to stay until an hour before dawn so they could leave under cover of darkness.

So engrossed in their work, the two groups had no idea that two challenging situations were beginning to unfold which would change their schedule, thus reducing their time at the sites and which would reveal who they were.

First, Erick was beginning to wake up, and secondly, Glenn's dog, Toby, was also waking up as he needed to go outside to relieve himself.

Toby entered Glenn's room, jumped on his bed and licked Glenn's face to awaken him. At the same time, Toby, who was sensitive to his surroundings, both in and outside of the house, began to realize something was wrong outside. He started to whine.

In the truck Erick had awakened and couldn't believe what he saw. Several flashlights could be seen through the keeper's house windows. When Erick looked towards the lighthouse, he could see many flashlights shining through its windows. As Erick looked back towards the keeper's house, he also saw a light turn on at Glenn's house and could also hear Toby barking. Erick grabbed his phone, which finally was working, and dialed Glenn.

"Hello Glenn, this is Erick. I'm sitting in my truck in front of the keeper's house. I couldn't get out of here because of the rain. I don't know why your light went on. It could be dangerous for you to go out. There are many people searching inside the lighthouse and keeper's house. They may be armed and dangerous if they see you or me."

"Erick, I have to take Toby out to relieve himself, but I'll take him to the backyard, then come right back. If you don't feel safe in your truck, why don't you sneak up here and I'll let you in the back door."

Erick said he would be right there. It was better for them to be together. Quietly, he opened and closed the truck door, then leaning over so not to be seen as he ran, he got to Glenn's back door. Glenn was waiting and held the door for him. Toby was becoming more excited. Toby knew something more than just a visit by Erick was happening.

"Glenn, why don't we turn off the lights, sit in the dark, and watch what's going on. Make sure all the windows and doors are locked. I'll help you."

When they had checked everything, they sat by two large front windows. Toby calmed down when the lights were off and laid on the floor between their chairs.

Around 4:30 am Erick had a hard time believing what he saw. At the same time as if coordinated, figures carrying flashlights exited the keeper's house and the lighthouse. Both groups joined each other behind Erick's truck and walked in a large group down the road which led to the highway.

"That sure is something, Erick. I thought it would be over after you found the painting and put it safely in the bank. What would a group that large be looking for?"

"I don't know, Glenn, but whatever it is must be worth a fortune to have a group that size looking for it. They have to belong to a bigger organization to have been so coordinated. To tell you the truth, I was tempted to follow them, but I'm sure they were armed and that is also the reason that I warned you too. Groups like that won't stop at murder if someone has witnessed what we saw. Until we get to the bottom of this, you, Glenn, have to be very careful. I and Maddie have to be careful too. But, now, more than ever, I want some great detective work done."

Then, Erick remembered Dan Ford, the FBI agent.

"Glenn, I'm going to introduce you to a very special person who can help us. But, one thing I don't want to do is to tell the Sheriff right now until I ask that very special person who you will be meeting soon."

"Erick, my lips are sealed, but what about Brad. When he gets here, his construction crew will see the mess."

Erick told Glenn he was going to act surprised since anyone could be a suspect. The group could have a local contact and, hopefully not, it could be a man on Brad's crew.

Erick checked his watch. It was 6:00am. Maddie would probably be up for the morning, so he dialed the inn. Heidi answered the phone then transferred it back to Maddie's apartment.

She answered.

"Erick, I'm so glad you called. I was really worried about you. Where have you been?"

Erick explained the whole story and assured her that he, Glenn, and Toby were safe.

"Maddie, I'm staying here all day to clean up and look around to see if I can find out what they were looking for."

"Erick, after the breakfast hour is finished, I'm coming to help you."

"One thing more, Maddie, do you have Dan Ford's number? I'm going to tell him what happened. I think right now only Dan and Glenn are the only ones we can believe. This is not a small group of people, but a large organization, perhaps even a cartel of sorts. We are up against something big and we have to know who is on our side."

Maddie gave Erick Dan Ford's number and said she would get to the Shipwreck Coast by noon.

Erick immediately called Dan and explained the situation. He told Erick that after his research, he had suspected this was bigger than they knew, and he would try to get to the Shipwreck Coast by mid afternoon. Dan agreed with Erick that they shouldn't tell anyone else including the Sheriff since stories like these fall into the grapevine immediately, especially in small towns.

After Glenn had fixed a hearty breakfast of Pancakes, eggs and bacon, coffee and juice, Erick left for the keeper's house. The floor was still cluttered with construction debris but had been shuffled around. There were dirt smudges, scrapes and dents left by the group of men who had poked everywhere including the ceiling and all the rooms.

Erick had been working on the fireplace and its tile surround. Fortunately, that had been left alone. It didn't look like they had found anything which meant they would be back. Erick interpreted that to mean it had turned into a very dangerous situation.

Erick remembered finding the painting. It had not been inside the house, but down a twenty foot shaft under a retaining wall which was hidden by a big flowery vine. Only Erick, Maddie, and Glenn knew about that hiding place. Erick hadn't seen any other treasure when he was at the bottom of the shaft where the painting was. Figuring that people would not hide all their treasures in one place, there must be something else on the property somewhere. Erick would have to put on his thinking cap and use his imagination as he searched in both buildings and other places on the property. His search would be camouflaged by his construction work. He could do both at the same time.

Maddie arrived promptly at noon with a brown bag lunch and drinks for both of them. Erick gave Maddie a hug and suggested they eat on Glenn's porch. After they climbed the steps to his door, Maddie tapped on his door to let him know they were there. Glenn welcomed them, but said he was involved with something, however, Toby would stay with them.

Toby and Maddie had bonded so he sat next to her and looked longingly at her food.

"Maddie, I hope with Dan's help we can solve this quickly. You are in great danger wherever you are, even at the inn. You and the inn are being spied on. I guess they know your every move, and I am betting on the fact that Mark Bronson was in that group last night."

As they were finishing their lunch a car pulled up next to Glenn's house. It was Special Agent Dan Ford. Erick signaled for him to join them on the porch.

"Would you like something to drink Agent Ford?"

"Thanks, but I think I'm good. So, tell me what's going on here."

For the next half hour, Erick explained the happenings of the previous night.

"Why don't you show me both the keeper's house and the lighthouse. Don't tell your workers in either place who I am. Just say I'm a friend."

As Dan Ford walked through the two buildings, he looked for places where someone could hide a valuable. He had gone through this procedure so many times that he knew what to look for, at least most of the time. He knew there were so many ways to hide rooms or small places which could hide items like gems or jewelry or silverware which no one knew about. He checked the steps and stairways in each place. Sometimes a step opens in a peculiar way to act as a small storage box. Then, with a carpet runner over the stairs, no one would be the wiser.

Dan told Erick about special small hiding places for small valuables and suggested he research these. Some could have been used in either the keeper's house or the lighthouse. He gave Erick and Maddie a smattering of ideas such as false bottom drawers, paint cans and tennis balls that had slits for an almost invisible opening to form a perfect hiding place for gems. There were fake wall outlets for jewelry and cash, a secret log box that really looks like a real log, or one could use a big box book that looks like a a real book on a book shelf mixed with real books.

Dan told Erick and Maddie there was a multitude of ideas for hiding places, so as he cleans up the keeper's house, to look closely at everything and every small item. These things or valuables could have been hidden for years as people in the past were almost more interested in thinking of ideas for hiding places than people are today.

"I'll keep in touch, Erick and Ms. Kirkpatrick, and if they come back another night to look for treasures, call me immediately even if it is three o'clock in the morning. They are very dangerous people. And one more item, I highly recommend you change your locks again, and only give your key to one person you trust."

Once Dan Ford had left, Maddie and Erick returned to cleaning the keeper's house. As Maddie was sweeping up the debris, Erick focused on his work with the fireplace. Both looked at every little thing with the possibility of being a hiding place.

Erick then left Maddie at the house and went to check on the lighthouse. He planned on walking up to the observation deck to check every nook and cranny along the way to make sure they were real rather then a hiding place posing as something else. He ran into Brad on the deck.

"I'm glad you're here, Erick. When I arrived this morning, it seemed as if someone had been in here last night. A lot of things were out of place particularly our construction materials. Did you see anyone around here?"

"No, Brad. I had to sleep in my truck. The rain and wind were so strong I couldn't leave. The storm left a lot of debris and supposedly the streets were flooded, but please keep an eye out for anything strange and let me know."

"Thanks, Erick, I will, and please tell Maddie I need to talk to her about the lighthouse. We are about to finish the bedrooms, and need to know paint colors, and about the white picket fence she wants to put on the lake side of the lighthouse, and what type of patio she wants out there by the lake."

The phone rang at the keeper's house and Maddie answered.

"Hello, Ms. Kirkpatrick, this is Oscar from the furniture store in Sault Ste. Marie. We are ready to ship your items and need the address."

Maddie gave him the address on the Shipwreck Coast and he informed her they would be there around noon the next day. She then remembered the area carpet she had bought and hoped they could deliver that before the furniture arrived. The carpet store gave her a 10 am arrival time.

Erick reminded Maddie that Dan Ford suggested they immediately change the locks on the two buildings. This time, Maddie decided to use a locksmith outside the area and scheduled an appointment with a company in Marquette, Michigan about one hour away. Erick and Maddie decided to tell no one about the new locks and since Erick would spend the nights at the keeper's house once the furniture arrived, he could unlock the lighthouse in the morning before Brad and the construction crew arrived.

Chapter 45

Her alarm rang at 6 am awakening Maddie from a deep sleep. Since she and Erick hadn't returned to the inn until 8pm the night before, she still felt exhausted as she dragged herself out of bed. The day ahead would be busy with the furniture deliveries, and the locksmith arrival.

After a warm shower, and hearty breakfast, Maddie updated Matt on her schedule for the day where she would spend her time at the Shipwreck Coast. Erick joined them at the front desk and said he was on his way to the keeper's house.

"I'll be there, Erick, before 10 am since the carpet for the front bedroom is scheduled to be delivered."

Maddie's drive to the Shipwreck Coast actually soothed her and she couldn't wait to see how the new furniture would transform the front bedroom. She had remembered to take sheets, blankets, pillows and a mattress pad in case Erick wanted to begin his time living there. She had also packed a cooler of sandwiches and drinks.

Arriving about a half hour before the carpet delivery, she checked the front bedroom and mopped the hardwood floor one last time. Erick was still working on the fireplace. The carpet van arrived a few minutes before 10 am. Once the men had positioned the carpet on the floor, the room immediately felt different. Even the sound of conversation in the room had changed from an echo sound to a normal conversation sound. Coziness was beginning to take shape.

The Marquette locksmith arrived on the heels of the carpet people. Mr. Taylor examined the present lock.

"Why are you changing this. It's new and this is one of the better locks."

Maddie explained about the break-ins and that someone must have duplicated the keys.

"This time, there will be only three of us who have keys."

The locksmith thought for a minute, then continued, "It sounds like you're in the market for some kind of restricted key since you are looking for security over convenience. You probably want to know how you can keep any other persons from copying your keys. So, there is a protected key system called 'Loc Doc Security.' It is offered through Medeco. If you get a Medeco key, the only way additional copies can be made is by requesting it through us. No other locksmith has access to our records, keys or systems. This means that when we get a request for key duplication, the person requesting is checked and validated through proper authorization on the account before any additional copies are made.

You will get what we call Security of Key Blanks which means that your keys are patented and restricted. No other locksmith can get the information or blanks to your locks. To even get a key blank you must go through the vendor."

The locksmith continued to explain that Maddie would have duplication control which means anyone could not just walk in to a Lowes or Home Depot and copy her keys in a machine. Only he, the locksmith, could cut keys for Maddie or for anyone she had personally authorized to request the keys.

Then, he continued to explain there is something called the Audit Trail which means he, the locksmith, keeps track of key requests and how many keys have been copied. Also, since he is the only vendor who has access to her blank keys, and if a key is lost or unaccounted for he can quickly get an audit trail of who is responsible for the loss and which keys are missing.

"So, Ms. Kirkpatrick, with our system you will have a patented key system that is protected by law from unauthorized duplication. My last question to you, is this the system that will make you feel safer as you work or live in these buildings?"

Maddie didn't have to think very long. She had never heard of such a security system, but had heard of Medeco and only positive things about the brand.

"It sounds fine to me, so let me show you the locks which need to be made more secure."

As Maddie showed the locksmith the doors to the keeper's house, then onto the lighthouse door, she figured Brad would see her and the locksmith's truck with the company's name on it and would question what was going on. Just as she had suspected, Brad had noticed her and Mr. Taylor's truck. After showing Mr. Taylor around the outside of the lighthouse, he returned to work on the keeper's house keys.

"So, what's up Maddie? Has something happened to your locks?"

"Well Brad, as you know, we've had some break-ins at night recently. We don't know what they're looking for, but I am getting locks that are way more secure. I'm not going to issue keys to many people, but Erick will be here before you and your crew arrive in order to open up the lighthouse and keeper's house."

"Sounds like you suspect someone on my crew."

"No, Brad, that's not it. I really think it is from an outside group, but we have to be very careful until we find out what's going on. Don't worry, you won't be inconvenienced."

Maddie then went to see Glenn. She informed him of the new locks and asked him if he would be the keeper of the third key. He could keep it in his safe.

"You can count on me, Maddie. I won't tell anyone I have it."

"Thanks, Glenn, that's a good idea. I don't want you to be in danger. Erick, you and I will keep this between us."

Maddie's cell phone rang. It was the furniture company's truck driver who said he was about fifteen minutes away.

When the truck arrived, Maddie directed it to the parking space closest to the keeper's house. The front bedroom had been freshly painted a few days before in a light gray with white trim which highlighted the beautiful light blue area rug. The furniture men placed the king size bed against an interior wall across from two windows looking out on the lawn between her house and Glenn's. The small chest fit between the two windows. Only one bedside table fit next to the bed, so Maddie decided to use the other table in a guest bedroom. At the last minute she bought a couple of lamps. One was placed on the small chest of drawers and the other was a floor lamp that she placed on one side of the bed. A full length mirror was hung next to the side of one of the windows.

After the furniture truck left, Maddie made the bed for Erick. She stood back when finished and realized she couldn't wait to furnish the rest of the rooms. Now that they had the new locks and a room for Erick, she felt as though all would fall into place quickly and they would be safe.

While she was admiring the new bedroom, Erick was checking the fireplace. The beautiful brick covering the inside of the fireplace needed cleaning, then there should be a safety check by an inspector on how safe it would be once they were finally able to light a fire. Erick had already finished polishing the beautiful tile on the fireplace surround. Erick had learned a lot about fireplace surrounds which was the term for the entirety of the fireplace excluding the fire box. It created the beauty of the fireplace including the mantel, hearth and legs surrounding the fireplace. He had enjoyed polishing all that was part of the fireplace surround. The fire box, however, was a different situation as it was a dirty job.

Maddie found Erick as he was brushing the inside of the fire box and beginning to inspect the integrity of the bricks.

"Are you willing to spend the night here, Erick, or do you need to return to the inn for your personal things?"

"So, my love, are you kicking me out already?"

"Not at all, but I thought you wanted to guard our house. I have to go back to the inn for a night to check on the staff, but will pack a bag and return tomorrow to stay with you. And remember, since we are the only ones, except for Glenn, who have the new keys, you'd have to be here early to unlock the buildings."

"Okay, I'll stay. At least we have running water so I can take a shower. After working on this firebox, I'll need one. Also, Glenn is alone and at least I can watch over him in case the mob returns. I also have my friend here", he said as he patted his holster and gun which hung from his waist.

Erick turned and hugged Maddie, "I'll miss you and can you pack some of my things, especially my razor or do you want me to grow a beard?"

"The beard is up to you, my love. Do you want to go out to dinner before I leave. If so, let's go to the little Italian restaurant in town, but I should leave well before dark."

They waited for the construction crew to leave, then locked the doors on the keeper's house and lighthouse before going to dinner.

As Maddie drove back to the Inn, she still had a nagging feeling that there was a connection she hadn't figured out between the event that had happened since getting the lighthouse and the strange and dangerous happenings. There was an under current of something that hadn't been solved and she could feel danger around her. She just had the feeling that she should always be vigilant and continually watch her surroundings. Lately, she felt wired most of the time which was exhausting.

She arrived at the inn just as dusk was turning to the pitch dark of the night. Heidi had already gone to her room and Matt was checking reservations to see how many guests were expected to arrive.

"Hey, Maddie, welcome back. It looks like the inn is full tonight, but I'll stay until 10pm. Since the town is quiet, I'm guessing any guests who are in town will be back soon, then we can call it a night."

Maddie went straight to her apartment to check her messages. The light was blinking showing that there were three messages. Two were from suppliers and one from Agent Dan Ford urging her to call him as soon as possible.

Agent Ford was glad to hear from Maddie.

"I know, Ms. Kirkpatrick, that you know we have a very dangerous situation here. I talked to the FBI's Art and Antiquity Crime department and there has been a movement in your area stretching from Sault Ste. Marie, Michigan and its sister town in Ontario, Canada towards the Shipwreck Coast of groups known for art theft. It also includes theft of other types of artifacts and valuables. They work all over the United States, but for some reason they have honed into your part of the country. The attempted art thefts in Minneapolis are a wing of this group. It is almost as if someone is feeding them information or leads as to where they can find valuable treasures, and they don't wait to pounce. They are not finished with you."

Maddie told him Erick was staying at the keeper's house and she would join him tomorrow to help with cleaning, painting and whatever needs to be done. She also informed him that they had just had new locks installed and she followed his advice and gave the third key to Glenn.

"I can assure you, Agent Ford, we are looking closely at every nook and cranny."

"Well, since this town is only about one hour from the Shipwreck Coast, I think, Ms. Kirkpatrick, I'll take a room at a hotel near your lighthouse in case they return and we will have to find a way for you to contact me in an emergency. In fact, I have a device I can put on your phone, but will meet you tomorrow to install it. I'll meet you at the Shipwreck Coast around noon. These groups usually don't strike in the morning or early afternoon, so until then stay safe."

"Oh, and one more thing, I know your painting is safe in the bank, but I can guarantee you they know that too. These groups are so large, they have eyes everywhere. You should warn the bank in the event they pose as someone who says you gave them the authority to pick up the painting for you."

I'm also going to assign an FBI agent to be a presence in the bank."

Maddie told him the painting was at the National Bank in Munising, Michigan and he should ask for Katie.

By the time her phone call with Agent Ford had ended, Maddie was shivering with fear. She took a couple of sleep assisting pills. The next day could be a dangerous day.

Her pills did the job and she actually slept for about six hours. As she slowly woke up, it only took a moment before she fully remembered what she might face. Maddie felt an urgency to talk to Erick. She realized that she hardly trusted anyone, so she didn't phone him and decided to talk to him in person back at the keeper's house.

On her way out, she pulled Matt aside and told him she might not be back for a few days because of problems at the lighthouse and keeper's house. She hinted that it could be dangerous so made sure he knew he was in charge and to call her if anything strange happened at the inn.

Arriving in Munising, her first stop was at the National Bank to alert them of Agent Ford's visit. Fortunately, Katie was there when she arrived. After explaining the situation to Katie, she emphasized, "Remember, if anyone comes into the bank saying they have my permission to get into my safety deposit box, please don't let them and call me immediately. I know they would have to have a key, but somehow with their background, they are brilliant at figuring out how to get what they want. They are a large group and they are very dangerous. At least Agent Ford will have one of his agents here with your permission."

As she pulled into the parking area in front of the keeper's house, she saw Erick walking through the glassed in breezeway towards the lighthouse. She ran over to the lighthouse to see what progress had been made. Brad met her and asked to have an appointment so she could choose more paint colors and the type of fencing she wanted and finally the landscaping for the yard facing Lake Superior. They decided to hold a meeting at four o'clock in the lighthouse. Erick would be there too.

After Erick checked a couple of steps on the spiral staircase, he and Maddie returned to the keeper's house.

"I want to show you what I have done to the fireplace."

He showed Maddie the polished tiles on the fireplace surround, and then the cleaning of the bricks which still needed more work.

"Whoever put the bricks on the back wall of the fireplace didn't do a great job. See how some of the bricks are a little different on the right side and not on the left. Most people will not notice it since they'll never be this close to the fireplace as I am, and I also think the flames would hide this flaw, especially in years gone by when whoever was living here probably had a fire everyday. Either way, I need to check on how strong they are."

Before Erick could continue, there was a knock at the door. It was Agent Ford.

"I've brought an alarm for both of you. I'm going to program it into your phones. It is so small that the piece with the button which you would push in an emergency is small enough to fit in any size pocket. It's silent so no one will know you've pressed anything and the sound will come through loud and clear on my phone. It will also send me a map of where you are, kind of like a GPS. So, if you could give me your phones, I'll go back to my car to program them."

Maddie looked at Erick then asked, "Do you think Glenn should have one?"

They both agreed to ask Glenn and when they called him, he was interested.

"Glenn, we don't know if Agent Ford has an extra one. If not, he will be staying in town and could probably have the FBI send an extra one to him. So, we'll let Agent Ford know you are interested. We three will be the only ones to have this protection, so no one should know about it."

Agent Ford returned with the two small devices. He demonstrated how to use them, then let each one try so they could hear the alarm and see the map. Before demonstrating, he made sure all doors and windows were closed. The sound of the alarm was ear piercing. The map on the agent's phone was clear and concise. Then Maddie suggested to him that Glenn was interested.

"Well, I think that is wise and I always bring a couple of extras with me, so I'll go up to the lodge now. After that, I will be at the Holiday Inn in Munising. Here is my card and direct number. You can call me anytime day or night."

Maddie called Glenn to alert him that Agent Ford was on his way to the lodge with the alarm.

"I feel so good that Glenn will be protected. I've always worried about him particularly with the danger I must have brought to this area after buying the lighthouse although I have no regrets about buying the lighthouse. I think it will be a great tourist attraction."

"Maddie, before I check that brick wall in the back of the fireplace, we need to lock the doors and windows."

After double checking and locking all entries into the house plus checking that all windows were closed and locked, Erick went to work poking and pushing the bricks on the right side of the fireplace wall. He felt a small sense of movement. As Maddie watched, Erick felt around the left side of the back fireplace wall which felt more solid. Going back to the right side, he played around with the bricks from top to bottom. At a single point not far from where the back wall met the brick ceiling, he felt a shifting. Putting both hands on that area and leaning in to put optimum strength on that area, he pushed to the left. There was a slight groan, then all of a sudden, three rows of brick at the top of the back wall and next to the right side wall of the fire box groaned again and shifted left uncovering a shelf behind the fireplace. A small safe sat on the shelf behind the fireplace. It had a combination lock. Because of his past career, Erick had become very good at listening to the clicks as he turned the lock slowly.

"Maddie, please get a paper and pen or pencil as I call out the numbers so you can write down the numbers when I turn the lock. I might have to try this several times. Something could be hidden in the safe."

When she returned with two notebooks, she told Erick she was ready. As he slowly started turning he called out, 'five,' then 'eleven,' then 'two.' There were a couple of other numbers he tried, then he asked to see the notebook to try different combinations. He would turn to a number, then turn the combination lock in the other direction past the first number to a second number then turn straight to a third number. Every time he tried a combination, Maddie, who had the second notebook would write it down. There were a couple of other number combinations he tried always using the same process. Maddie marked all the combinations in her notebook. The list of combinations was growing longer with no luck. Finally, Erick turned the lock in one direction to see if he could hear some clicks on numbers where he hadn't heard them. There were two possible numbers where he heard a click that he hadn't heard before. Maddie added the new numbers to her list as a new combination. Finally, a combination of the newest numbers worked and the door opened. Maddie marked those three numbers as the combination.

Inside was a small flowered box. The safe had kept it from aging. Opening the box they found a black velvet bag. Erick brought the bag out and gently put it on the kitchen table. They slowly and carefully opened it. Inside they found six loose gems. They were six emeralds. There was also a woman's brooch decorated with small gems.

Erick and Maddie looked at each other with disbelief.

"This must be the rest of the treasure. No wonder the mob couldn't find it the night they were here. Who's ever heard of bricks that can slide to reveal a hiding place with a safe."

"Remember, Erick, what we have learned in our search is that people from years ago were expert in hiding valuables by creating secret places."

"Do you think, Erick, that this has to do with the Joey story from World War II. Gems are so small they would be easy to mail. But our first priority is to immediately put the gems somewhere safe. I guess we can ask Glenn again if we can use his safe. He may know of a jeweler close by who could appraise the emeralds. But, first we need to close the safe and shove the bricks over to hide it."

Maddie phoned Glenn to ask if they could come over to his lodge. They needed his help.

When they were satisfied that the brick fireplace looked as though nothing special had happened or changed, they left for Glenn's lodge hoping the new locks on the keeper's house would keep it safe.

Glenn could hardly believe his eyes when he saw the gems and heard the story. He carefully locked them in his safe.

"Do you two think there is anymore treasure to find in the house or is this the end of the treasure."

"We have no idea, Glenn, but I hope so."

"Every time we find something else, the danger grows. And every time you very kindly help us hide it, the danger grows for you too which makes us very worried for you."

"You don't have to worry about me, Maddie. Toby will keep me safe and I do have a gun. All of us hunters have at least one."

"Glenn, do you know of any reputable jewelry appraisers around here?"

He thought for a moment, then replied, "Yes, I do. My late wife inherited some jewelry from her parents and went to an appraiser in Duluth. I'll get the number and you could give him a call."

Glenn left to find the information and returned with a business card which read John Sorenson of Sorenson Jewelers and Appraisers on Lake Street in Duluth.

Erick added, "I think we should drive to Duluth when you have an appointment, Maddie, so you and your stash of gems will be protected. I will have a gun too."

Maddie immediately phoned Sorenson's Jewelers and talked to John Sorenson just as he was closing for the day. They made an appointment for two days later at 2pm. Erick and Maddie decided to leave the next morning.

"Maddie, I'll be here all day so come over anytime to retrieve the gemstones."

"Again, thanks, Glenn so much for helping us again. You are a dear friend."

"Don't worry, Maddie, I won't tell anyone what's going on or where you are going."

Maddie phoned Matt at the Twin Sisters Inn saying she would be delayed at the Shipwreck Coast for a few days. She didn't mention where she was going, but knew Matt could always phone her. Both Erick and Maddie decided to spend the night at the Holiday Inn in Munising. It would be safer. Erick would have to open the keeper's house and lighthouse for the workers.

The next morning dawned with cloudy skies threatening rain. Maddie and Erick left around ten o'clock for the six hour drive to Duluth after stopping at Glenn's for the gemstones.

"Be careful, Glenn, and please if you see any strange people or happenings around my property please call. I want you to be safe too. And, thanks for using your keys to close up both buildings tonight and opening them for the workers tomorrow."

"Don't worry about it, Maddie, if you are not here I will open and close the buildings at the proper times."

CHAPTER 46

After their first night in Duluth, Maddie and Erick stayed close to the hotel. They put their gemstones in the room's safe. They ate breakfast in their rooms, and each got their breakfast separately so one of them would always stay in the room to watch the safe. They spent most of the day watching movies on the television. Maddie researched gemstones on her I Phone. She discovered that in some cases emeralds were worth more than diamonds.

She read that in South and Central America, particularly in Colombia, the cartels favored emeralds over diamonds since emeralds surpassed diamonds in value. That information made her feel more vulnerable. Could there be a cartel behind all that had happened to her?"

Despite her nervousness and concern about the gemstones, she slept well the second night and awoke to a sunny day with growing excitement for her meeting with John Soronson.

When she and Erick entered Soronson's Jewelers and Appraisers, her excitement peaked. Mr. Soronson was an older man in his mid sixties with a gentle kind demeanor. He escorted them to his office located downstairs from the main jewelry store. He had two sales people manning the jewelry store and asked them not to bother him unless there was an emergency'

Maddie presented him with the velvet bag containing the emeralds and the brooch.

Mr. Soronson took the gems over to a special table where there was a bright light. At first glance, Mr. Soronson was surprised that the gemstones were so natural with very few defects.

"I think you are looking at some very valuable gemstones, but first I must let you know that I am a certified gemologist so can act as an official appraiser of jewelry and complete appraisals that can be used for insurance purposes."

Mr. Sonronson laid out his jewelry tools, appraiser forms, precision microscopes and a jewelry caliper for measuring even the smallest stones and settings. There was also a gem scale, carat weight charts and a plastic tweezer for picking up the stones. He wore tight medical gloves.

"This may take some time, but if you really want to understand what you have, I urge you to stay and watch and I will explain what I am doing."

Mr. Soronson then explained that gemstones are graded based on the 'Four C's' of gem grading which stand for clarity, cut, and carat(weight). The gemstones are also graded by the rarity of their features.

"I will also look at the color by analyzing three properties—hue, tone, and saturation. Hues refer to the basic colors of red, orange, yellow, green, blue, violet and purple which are the basic colors of the rainbow. The black, white and brown refer to tones and saturation, not hues.

So, what are tones and saturation. The tones refer to the gemstone's lightness and darkness which means that black and white are tones from darkest to lightest. A gem's saturation refers to the intensity of the hue which can be strong or soft. For example, pink is desaturated red, and warm colors like red and orange become shades of brown as their saturation decreases."

Mr. Soronson then explained the color grades for high value colored gems.

"First, you are very lucky to have emeralds since they are rarer and often much more expensive than diamonds. In fact, it's reported that emeralds are twenty times rarer than diamonds which explains their extreme values."

He went on to explain that some of the most valuable emeralds come from Colombia, South America. That is because of the special geographical conditions in Colombia which produce exactly the slightly bluish green shade and strong saturation which makes those stones the epitome of the variety.

He explained that in Colombia there are two mines there, the Muzo and Chivor mines that produce these emeralds which are a little different from each other depending on which mine they come from. If they come from the Muzo mine, their material tends to be a yellowish green whereas if they come from the Chivor mine they have more of a blue green appearance. Emeralds with medium to medium dark tones are the most valuable, however the deep green gems are the most prized and expensive.

"So, after all this explanation, Ms. Kirkpatrick, I hope your head isn't spinning, but what you have here are some very valuable gemstones. I hope you have insurance, if not, you need to call your insurance agent immediately to get coverage before you leave this lab."

A chill went down Maddie's back, then she asked in a shaky voice, "What characteristics do you see in these gemstones, Mr. Soronson, that makes you think they are so valuable?"

He answered, "I can tell by their vivid green color they are most certainly from Colombia. They are not all the same size, but fairly close."

He pointed to two and after measuring them, found them to be around 3.8 carats. They were vivid green and they had characteristics from the Muzo mine deposit, so he estimated the two together would be around $ 50000.00 or more. Then he measured a set of larger emeralds which were also a vivid green and from Colombia and estimated them to be just under $ 100000.00. The last two emeralds were the largest. They were 4.0 carats. He checked the gemstones for inclusions. In an emerald, inclusions aren't necessarily bad. Mr. Soronson explained that in emeralds inclusions are viewed as desirable features since they form lovely patterns, referred in the trade as the emerald's jardin which is French for garden. They are so unique that they can actually increase the gemstone's value. These inclusions can be seen by the naked eye, so no specialist's equipment is required to assess a stone.

"You definitely have inclusions in this gemstone and their pattern is very graceful, so this should add to its value. I think the Gemology Society would probably rate this gem with five A's which is excellent, so I would appraise this around "$ 110,000.00."

The last gemstone was an oblong shape and was the biggest around 15.56 carats. Maddie had not noticed the huge size of the gemstone. As with the other emeralds, Mr. Soronson held it up to the light. Like the others it did not sparkle with fire, but it did with a dull fire, which is what real emeralds do. Mr. Soronson told Maddie and Erick if the emeralds did sparkle and have intense fire, they would likely be fake. All Maddie's emeralds had passed the test. They were very real and very valuable.

"So, Mr. Soronson, what do you think this oblong emerald is worth?"

"Ms Kirkpatrick, I would appraise this one around $ 130000.00. So, Ms. Kirkpatrick, if you add these appraisals up, you have a treasure here of almost a half a million dollars."

Since emeralds are becoming rare, their value should go up, so suggest you keep them somewhere very safe. You should call your insurance agent now."

"But, Mr. Soronson, did you see the brooch?"

He put on his glasses.

"Well, we can't miss this, but you should contact your insurance agent while I take a look at this, so the paper work can begin on the loose gems."

Maddie stepped into the next room to call Mike Thresher at Northern Insurance Co. while Erick stayed with Mr. Soronson.

The appraiser looked at the brooch. The edge around the brooch was decorated with very small diamond gemstones. The middle of the brooch displayed a medium sized emerald gemstone. The brooch was a locket and once opened, there was a message inscribed which was inscribed in gold and read, "I love you. We will be safe. Holland, 1935."

Maddie appeared in the doorway to to say that Mike Thresher, her insurance agent, was on the phone and wondered if Mr. Soronson had appraised the brooch.

"Ms. Kirkpatrick, add another fifty thousand dollars for the brooch. It is a World War II antique, so that would bring your policy to over a half a million dollars if you consider future inflation. Your agent should know."

Mike Thresher suggested going as high as a one million dollar policy which Maddie accepted. He suggested that she take pictures of the collection and keep the pictures and the appraisal in a separate safe place from the gems and brooch.

Erick and Maddie collected the gems and put them back in the small velvet bag with the brooch, then thanked Mr. Soronson and said they would be expecting his bill for the appraisal. They had not cancelled their hotel rooms in Duluth, so before returning to the Holiday Inn, they visited a Chinese Restaurant, ordered a carry out, then went back to the hotel. They locked their very valuable possessions in the safe which was located in the closet of Erick's room. They decided to check out of the hotel early the next morning to drive directly to the Northern Bank in Munising in order to rent a small safety deposit box for their treasure. Maddie would phone Katie at the bank to alert her that they needed another safety deposit box that day. If they had time to return to Sault Ste Marie the same day, they would after Erick received a construction update from Brad. Then, maybe they could find peace for a while.

The next afternoon as they parked their car in front of the bank, Maddie phoned Katie and asked her for the bank security agent to escort them from their car to the bank. Having the gems in her possession had Maddie almost shaking with fear. She carried the gems and brooch in a large purse strapped across her body. The straps were a combination of a chain and leather so was very sturdy.

Although they were successful in getting to and locking their valuables in one small safe deposit box, they were unaware that there was a telescope trained on them as they entered the bank. They decided to return to the bank the next morning to take pictures of the emeralds and rent another safe deposit box for the pictures before returning to Sault Ste. Marie.

The hidden spy was located in an office building across from the bank. Even though the spy had no idea what Erick and Maddie had, he knew it was valuable, especially when he had seen the appearance of the bank guard escorting them into the bank. He knew he had to immediately report this event to his group. Their plans were fluid and procedures were always changing. He also knew that furniture had recently been delivered to the keeper's house, so at least Erick would be living there around the clock. His group's nighttime raid there several days before had been witnessed by Erick and Glenn so the security around the house most surely had been tightened. He also knew about the painting and assumed there must have been more valuables discovered, so access to the lighthouse and keeper's house would be tricky, A new plan was beginning to formulate in his mind.

CHAPTER 47

"We're back", Maddie chimed as she and Erick entered the Twin Sisters Inn.

Matt and Heidi seemed happy that their boss had finally returned. No guests were at the front desk, so Maddie went over to get an update from Matt. All had remained normal during Maddie's absence.

Since work on the renovation of the lighthouse was progressing rapidly, Maddie phoned Shannon Kelly, a good friend and an interior and space designer who could help her pick out furniture, carpets and other decorating ideas for both the keeper's house and lighthouse. They scheduled a meeting for 4pm that afternoon.

While all was quiet in the late morning, Heidi began to finish some filing until her phone vibrated with the message, "We have to meet. I'll pick you up at noon for lunch. Be ready for a change." Heidi became very worried. Matt suggested that she take her lunch break at 12pm since she had worked so hard while Maddie was gone. He even gave her permission to take two hours for lunch. Her face lit up and she calmed down.

Once she had left, Matt buzzed Mattie to let her know that Heidi would be gone for two hours, so if she needed to talk to him alone, now would be the time. Within a few minutes Maddie joined him behind the desk. She had decided to tell him everything that had happened. He promised to tell Heidi nothing, but was amazed at the treasure she and Erick had found. Maddie also asked Matt to start considering where he would like to be General Manager—at the lighthouse or at the Twin Sisters Inn.

"In a few days, Matt, I am taking my designer, Shannon Kelly, to see the properties on the Shipwreck Coast, and would like you to look at them too as soon as we can find the time. There will be no pressure on you to decide. It's what will be most comfortable for you."

Maddie suddenly remembered that she hadn't informed Agent Ford of the gemstones, the newest treasure. Fortunately he answered his phone on the first ring. Listening quietly to Maddie's newest finding, he told her she was right to keep the gems very secure in the bank vault, and reminded her that now the danger around her, Erick and Glenn had just become stronger and to expect that whomever was after the treasure would strike soon and to remember they probably already knew about the gems.

"You three should keep your alarms on you at all times. Just push the button and I will be on the way. They will be watching you and following you wherever you go. I suspect their next attack will be near the lighthouse. Remember, I am staying in Munising so am close by."

Maddie informed Agent Ford that she and her designer would probably be there within a day.

Then, she decided to ask Matt to come with them but he would have to drive his own car and return that night if he didn't mind driving in the dark. She was taking a risk leaving Heidi alone but knew that Heidi was capable of handling the front desk by herself. Maddie would give her a bonus in her next paycheck.

The next day after returning to the Shipwreck Coast, the meeting with Shannon proved very fruitful with the designer offering many creative ideas. Matt was fascinated with the lighthouse and the keeper's house. The location with the lighthouse sitting at the top of a cliff over looking the lake was very intriguing to him.

CHAPTER 48

Heidi was excited to manage the inn alone for a day. Only she and the guests would be there. So, she checked some reservations and was relieved to see that she would have fewer guests at the inn than usual.

After about an hour when no guests were in the lobby, Heidi replied to the text which had informed her that there would be some changes. She seemed satisfied with the new turn of events and felt a confidence that she was now in charge of the inn. It was a perfect front for her.

The weather at the Shipwreck coast was clear and sunny, a perfect day for Shannon and Matt to get a feel for the property. Shannon took many pictures both of the interior and exterior. Since Shannon had followed Maddie and Erick in her car, she decided to return to Sault Ste Marie that night. Maddie was relieved that Shannon and Matt would not stay over night as she she felt an uneasy feeling of the danger growing around the group. She and Erick would stay in the keeper's house for a night or two, but first she had to bring Glenn up to date.

"I'm so glad, Maddie, that both you and Erick will be staying here for the next few days. So far, the nights have been quiet. No bad guys on the scene", Glenn chuckled.

"Well, I am sure, Glenn, they will be back soon. At least that is what Agent Ford thinks, and he is close by near Munising. And don't forget to keep your alarm with you at all times, Glenn.

And now I must return to the keeper's house. Have a good night, Glenn."

"See you tomorrow, Maddie, and enjoy all that new furniture which was just delivered."

As she approached the house, she realized that with the new lamp light shinning through the windows, the keeper's house had taken on a cozy and homey feel.

Erick surprised Maddie with a small television he had remembered to bring. There was an old cable outlet so he was able to connect the television and with one phone call to the cable company, the service was turned on. It wasn't picture perfect but they could at least enjoy it and the cable group promised to come and adjust everything within a few days.

The couple enjoyed dinner at their favorite Italian restaurant in town, then returned for their first night in the keeper's house.

"Maddie, I'm going to buy spotlights for this house and some for the lighthouse. At least we already have lights in the breezeway."

"And, Erick, I would feel safer if we keep the lamps on all night. I just feel that regardless of who these groups of people are, they will sneak up on us in the middle of of the night."

"Maddie, since they did that before, I'm not sure they'll do it again, but will have a different plan, so let's try to forget about it and go to bed."

Fortunately, Maddie fell into a deep sleep until seven am when the incessant ringing of the phone pierced her consciousness. Erick had already left to work in the lighthouse. Wondering who could be calling so early, she cleared her throat then answered the phone.

"Ms. Kirkpatrick, this is Dan Ford. I hope the first night in your house was a safe one. If you haven't turned on the news yet, you probably haven't heard that there was an attempted break-in at the Northern Bank in Munising. The perpetrators tried to blow open the vault where the safe deposit boxes are, but were unsuccessful and got away before the police arrived. So, you and Erick need to meet me this morning at my office since we will have to change our strategy and we need to do this immediately. Can both of you get to my office by 10am?"

"Certainly, Agent Ford, we'll be there."

At 10 am sharp, Maddie and Erick knocked on Agent Ford's door.

"Thank you for meeting me on such short notice. I think the break in at the bank last night was to get into your safe deposit boxes, Ms. Kirkpatrick, so here's what I propose. What I have in mind is going to be very risky and dangerous, but rather than waiting for them to attack us, we will have to coax them out into the open. To do this, I would like you to put an article in the town's newspaper announcing the progress you have made on turning the lighthouse and keeper's house into a B&B. Even though the construction on this project has not been completed, you can say that you're planning on having a preliminary open house so the town can see what it looks like and then, with drawings of what it will be like when it is finished and ready to open for business. At that time, you will have a second open house to advertise the completed B&B to the public. You should also add that during the construction, a valuable historic painting was found and it will be on display.

Remember, I told you about the security display case which can be used and I know where I can get one for you. We will figure out when to install it. Then, the night before the first open house, we will make arrangements with the bank to let you in after closing so you can retrieve the painting from your safe deposit box. Then, under cover of darkness, we will transfer it to the case in your home. I will be with you all the time during the transfer to your house, and, of course will be armed. I will probably ask my agent who has been at the bank everyday to also accompany us.

During the open house, I won't be by the painting, but will be nearby. Probably, you or Erick should stand by the display case so you can explain the history."

"I suppose, Agent Ford, you want the first open house to be in the next few days?"

"Yes, as soon as possible, Ms. Kirkpatrick."

Erick looked at Maddie, then back at Agent Ford, "I think we can pull this off, but Agent Ford, do you think they will try something during the open house or after?"

"Erick, they will have seen it in the paper, and maybe you could put some flyers up around the town, so they will have enough time to plan. They may come in towards the end of the open house when most people have left."

"When you two write your article for the newspaper, and the flyer, please let me check it before you make it public."

"What time of day should we plan the open house, Agent Ford?"

"I would do it on a Saturday afternoon between two to five pm. And one more thing, let your Sheriff know about the open house but not about me or our plan. Just make sure he knows that it is only to show the town's people the progress you are making and to look forward to the completed project which will be on display at the second open house."

After checking her calendar, Maddie suggested holding the first open house a week from Saturday which would give them about ten days to prepare.

"Fine, then, tell me when you have fixed up the house so I can check it. I will talk to your bank tomorrow."

Erick told Maddie he would talk to Brad about the open house so he and his workers wouldn't have to stop their work. He was sure that Brad would act as the tour guide for the lighthouse since he also knew the history of the surrounding area including the history of the lighthouse.

CHAPTER 49

A week of concentrated work on the keeper's house and lighthouse passed quickly. Although many areas were still under construction, Maddie had brought in other furniture she had acquired to make more than the master bedroom look comfortable and livable. She had even been able to put some cottage looking curtains in the dining room-living room combination plus adorning the windows in the guest rooms. She had quickly spread area rugs in the guest rooms, and covered the temporary beds with beautiful handmade quilts some of which had designs and pictures of the Shipwreck Coast. She had also finished her article for the paper announcing the first open house.

With Agent Ford's permission, they delayed the open house for an extra week of promotion so the public would have time to read and digest the newspaper article and to see the flyers she had stapled or taped to various trees, poles, or whatever she could find around town. After all, they were advertising the open house in Sault Ste Marie and in the Munising area including other parts of the Shipwreck Coast.

When they were finished, she phoned Agent Ford. Upon his arrival, he seemed very pleased with their work and also brought the security display box for the painting.

"So, we have two days until the open house. I'll contact Katie at the bank and make arrangements to come in at 3:00 am on Saturday morning. Before then, I will install the security display box in the hall by the stairs facing the front door for all to see as they enter the foyer."

Maddie mentioned that as she was hanging the flyers around town, she went to the Sheriff's office to leave him a copy and to explain the reason for the open house.

"I never mentioned to the Sheriff the real reason for the open house other than to introduce our project to the town."

Maddie told Matt and Heidi about the open house but that they should stay at the Twin Sisters Inn and she would give them a private tour later.

The few days before the open house, it seemed as though time passed in slow motion, but finally Friday arrived, then early Saturday morning. Katie had said that she would meet Agent Ford and Erick at the front door of the bank at 3 am. Maddie stayed behind after giving Erick her key to the safe deposit box.

Both Agent Ford and Erick and Ford's FBI bank agent were armed. They met Katie at the front door. Katie had left some low lights on near the vault.

"So, Katie, what does your bank management think of this?" Ford said in a low voice.

"Don't worry, Agent Ford, they know all about it, and after that explosion and attempted robbery several days ago, they are all for you being here and hope you will get to the bottom of this situation."

She led them to Maddie's box where they retrieved the painting and gently put it in an insulated box which supplied a lot of cushioning around the painting. After locking the box and closing the vault, Katie turned off the lights and silently led them out of the bank.

"Are you going to be okay, Katie, going to your car?"

"Yes, but it would make me feel safer if one of you come with me to my car."

Agent Ford thought a moment, then answered, "Why don't you come with us and we will drive you to your car and wait until you are safely on your way since we three should not split up."

She was fine with that. After they had inspected her car and the inside of the trunk, they knew Katie was safe, but to be sure, they all left at the same time. Erick, Agent Ford and the FBI agent followed her in their cars to ensure that no other person was following her. Erick and Agent Ford then returned to the keeper's house.

After Dan Ford had securely hung the painting in the display cabinet and tested the lock, he stood back. Maddie flipped the switch on the cabinet light. As all three gazed at the painting, they were amazed at the life it brought into the foyer.

"Remember, this is the most secure display cabinet on the market. Museums use them for their most valuable treasures. It is virtually impossible to break the glass."

"But Agent Ford, some thieves have broken into them, right?"

"Ms. Kirkpatrick, that is true but they'd have to steal the whole cabinet and I have secured the cabinet to the wall with special locks. If they tried to smash it in as it hung on the wall, a siren would go off just like it would if they tried to steal the whole cabinet. This glass breaks from the inside out, so they would have to figure out how to implode it from the inside, but then the painting would be destroyed. I also think they would not want to draw attention to themselves."

Agent Ford also suggested that he keep the keys to the cabinet until they had the situation under control.

"Thanks, Agent Ford, and since it is not long before morning dawns, would you like to stay for a snack?"

"That is very kind of you, Ms. Kirkpatrick, but I need to get back to the office.

Perhaps back there I can catch a quick 'shut eye' before starting a new day. I will be back for the open house and will linger in the background. I suggest you two get some rest also."

Shortly before 2pm, Brad Elstad knocked on the front door. As Erick invited him in he exclaimed, "Wow, where did you get that beauty. The painting looks phenomenal in this location."

Erick answered, "It was one of the treasures that came with the property."

"You always luck out, Erick. Anyway, my guys are working hard on the lighthouse, and I am ready to be your tour guide whenever anyone shows up. A lot of people are not familiar with all the functions a lighthouse can achieve, so I will make the tour as educational as possible."

Maddie answered, "And I am going to stand by the painting in the foyer while Erick will be the tour guide for the keeper's house. We will also have a big sign in front of the keeper's house with the announcement, "Welcome, Your Tour Begins Here At The Keeper's House."

"Since I see some cars arriving, we should all take our places.

The first guests were couples followed by Agent Ford who played the part of a tourist before taking a chair in the main room where he had a full view of the painting and the guests as they entered and wandered around the house.

Maddie informed the guests that there was also a tour guide at the lighthouse and she pointed out through her windows facing the lighthouse the breezeway which connected the keeper's house to the lighthouse so they wouldn't have to walk over the lawn which could be damp. She also warned them not to go too close to the top of the cliff on the lake side of the lighthouse since they had not installed the planned fence around the backyard or lakeside of the lighthouse. Maddie had installed warning signs near the top of the cliff to stay back several feet and she asked that they keep their children safe from the cliff. She had also installed a decorative rope encircling the back yard with warning signs attached to them. A few colorful balloons attached to the rope added a festive party feeling as they swayed back and forth in the constant wind from Lake Superior.

There were colorful Adirondack chairs by the back wall of the lighthouse so the guests could enjoy the view of Lake Superior.

Servers were passing around trays holding glasses of champagne. A few tables holding hors d'oeuvres were placed strategically off to one side of the backyard. As Brad finished his lighthouse tour with each group, he led them to the backyard for drinks and hors d'oeuvres.

As the afternoon began to wind down, one last guest arrived—the Sheriff.

"Good afternoon, Ms. Kirkpatrick. I decided to check on the progress of your B&B. You have really finished a lot since the last time I was here. And, that painting in your foyer is quite a prize. Did you find it in some nook and cranny around here?"

"Hardly, Sheriff, but it is a long story. I plan on researching its historical background."

The Sheriff walked over to get a closer look at the painting.

"This is some special display box you have. It looks very secure."

"We're just trying to keep everything safe around here, Sheriff."

Agent Ford was watching the Sheriff closely from the side of the room. He realized that as a Sheriff, he should be interested in special cabinets particularly if they had certain security features, and especially if he had been involved in cases involving art or artifact theft. Agent Ford slowly got up and walked over to the Sheriff.

"Who are you", the Sheriff asked."

"I'm just a tourist who is passing through your town and when I saw the signs for the new bed and breakfast, I decided to check it out. It has a unique location on top of the cliff over looking one of the Great Lakes. I also have friends who vacation in this area so I am checking it out for them. You seem to be interested in the special cabinet. You must have contacts in the world of artifacts."

"Oh no, I haven't had much experience in art. The people of our town have to go to the big city museums if they have an interest in art."

Maddie interrupted, "Sheriff, when you are finished touring the keeper's house, don't forget to see the lighthouse. My construction crew is doing a wonderful job. Also, when you are there, checkout the backyard, or as we call it, the lakeside of the lighthouse with a beautiful view of Lake Superior.

We have refreshments too."

As soon as the Sheriff left, Agent Ford turned to Maddie, "There's something about that guy. I know he's the Sheriff, and maybe he was trying to be polite, but he certainly had an interest in the painting, and especially, the display cabinet and how secure it is. I'll keep my eyes on him."

"Agent Ford, now that this open house is coming to an end, how safe do you think we'll be?"

"Things will become more dangerous since the painting has gone public. This is why you and Erick need to keep your alarms on you at all times even when you are sleeping."

"Agent Ford, I know you are staying at the Holiday Inn in Munising, but if its okay with Glenn, I would feel safer if you could stay overnight at his house. You could hide your car behind his house."

As Maddie knocked on Glenn's door, she realized she hadn't seen him at the open house.

"Well, how's my neighbor? Did you have many guests at your open house?"

"Why didn't you come Glenn. We missed you. And you missed our refreshments of champagne and yummy hors d'oeuvres" on the lake side of the lighthouse."

"I really wanted to, Maddie, but I thought it might be better if I stayed up here on my porch guarding your place. Remember, I have Toby. I did not see anyone suspicious or loitering around, but was surprised that the Sheriff came. He has seemed so indifferent to what has been going on around here as if he is distracted."

After being asked, Glenn said that Agent Ford was always welcome to stay the night.

"Thanks Glenn, and Erick and I will bring up the extra champagne and hors d'oeuvres for you to sample. You won't have to eat dinner after that. They are very filling."

Agent Ford reluctantly gave in.

"Ms. Kirkpatrick, I can only stay one night with Glenn as I have to get back to my office the first thing in the morning, but please stay vigilant."

Chapter 50

Surprisingly, the night was quiet and uneventful. Maddie felt that whoever was trying to give her a false sense of security had probably planned it that way. Trying not to dwell on the danger, she decided to stay busy. Most of the party dishes needed to be washed although she planned on keeping the backyard decorations up as they made the yard so festive. She turned on the radio to keep her company.

The weather segment had just begun and the announcer was warning of another strong storm moving across Lake Superior scheduled to hit in the late afternoon. An alert had gone out to the ships particularly to those who might be sailing in the Shipwreck Coast area during that time. They were advised to either increase their speed to get through the area ahead of the storm or to find one of the coves for shelter. The storm was expected around 4:30pm, so Maddie informed her construction crew and advised Brad he should let them go home early since the roads had a reputation for flooding. Reluctantly, she removed the party's backyard decorations behind the lighthouse.

Agent Ford had also heard about the storm, and was glad he had returned to his office.

His main office had called to advise him that the group they were surveilling, which he thought was connected to the spying and vandalism on Maddie's property, were taking a new course of action by connecting and coordinating with other like groups. They would be larger and more powerful and dangerous now.

Maddie contacted Glenn to inform him of the storm.

"Well, Maddie, we're going to have to 'batten down the hatches' as it is expected to be a violent one. I'm fine up here. My house is very solid. How about you."

"Erick and I are okay down here. If you need anything please contact us."

Maddie's last chore was to find candles and place her hurricane lamps around the house and in the enclosed breezeway. She then walked to the lighthouse to find out when the guys were leaving. She knew Erick would lock up as soon as the crew left. She decided to wait for him and watch the storm come in while she sat in one of the Adirondack chairs overlooking Lake Superior. She could see the storm arriving in the distance from the west. For a few minutes there was the orange glow of the sun setting which in very rapid fashion was blacked out by the approaching angry dark clouds. The thunder heard in the distance would soon by upon them.

The wind was whipping the waves into a frenzy. They were high and powerful with huge white caps. When Maddie walked to the edge of the cliff, she could see the waves had obliterated the beach below and were washing up to the bottom of the cliff.

In the distance she could see the lights of a freighter which had passed the Shipwreck Coast in the nick of time. The freighter must have been traveling at excess speed as its lights rapidly became little dots of light in the distance then disappeared from sight.

"At least one ship got through", she thought. She hoped the other freighters had anchored in some of the coves and inlets to the west.

As she looked over the cliff's edge, she saw some small but seemingly strong trees growing on the side of the cliff to her right. They must have begun their growth out of some crevice.

Maddie thought the trees must be very strong to have survived these storms which were plentiful in the summer and fall. There was no beach as far as her eyes could see to the west or to the east toward Sault Ste. Marie. The sound of thunder was becoming louder as if to herald the storm's arrival. Large steaks of lightning cut across the sky.

Erick shouted from the lighthouse, "How long are you going to stay out there? The storm's getting close. I'm going to the house and the guys have left before the streets flood."

"I'll be back soon", she shouted. Then continued, "Please fill the bathtub with water just in case there is a problem with the well or utilities."

Maddie had forgotten to bring a flashlight since the sun had been out when she arrived at the cliff. Before she knew it, darkness had prematurely settled over the land. Some storms can turn the day into nighttime in a few minutes even in the middle of the day, but this one was arriving at the end of the afternoon.

Glancing one last time at the churning water and the lost beaches, she turned and headed towards the breezeway as large water drops began to fall. Before she could reach the breezeway, pelting, stinging drops of rain hit her face at all angles. She turned on the lanterns in the breezeway where she was protected from the storm. As she walked through the glass enclosure she saw lightning strikes on all sides. The fury of the storm was approaching quickly and she knew from the weather forecast that it may stall for a time around the Shipwreck Coast.

She could see the hurricane lanterns glowing through the windows of the keeper's house adding a feeling of coziness and protections from the frenzy outside. Maddie glanced at Glenn's house. His lights were on and all seemed to be okay. At least, they all had each other.

To her, Glenn was the uncle she never had and would always be there for her.

As she entered the house from the breezeway, she could smell the aroma of Erick cooking steaks. There were small potatoes, zucchini and Merlot wine. At least the electricity had not gone off.

Just as they sat down for the dinner, the electricity blinked a few times then went out.

Their battery operated special storm radio announced that electricity was off all over the area. Maddie and Erick didn't care. Their lanterns cast a romantic hue over their dinner.

"I sure hope Glenn is okay, and Toby must be going crazy. All dogs do during storms."

They had just finished dinner and were enjoying the rest of the wine when there was a thump sound outside their door. Erick looked out but couldn't see anything, so keeping the chain on the front door, he peeked out. No one was there, but a few tree branches had come down and were rolling around their yard.

They went to the living room to finish their wine and to listen to the storm updates. So far, the storm was malingering over the Shipwreck Coast. As they sat in their living room, Erick and Maddie could never have imagined what was happening at the bottom of the cliff.

With no lights on, a private small yacht had pulled up to the bottom of the cliff. Several figures dressed in black waded through the churning water to the bottom of the cliff. With ropes in their hands, they methodically threw their ropes forward to attach onto the limbs of the small trees growing on the sides of the cliff. The lightning streaks which lighted up the sky allowed them to see where to throw their ropes so they would land on the limbs of the stronger trees and they would be able to pull on the ropes in order to climb the cliff. All of them had been trained for these situations. Their training had been comparable to military training and they had practiced for months. The only difference was they were after a treasure, not a person or enemy. But, if anyone got in their way, they would be considered collateral damage. Their treasure was a valuable or maybe valuables that were worth a lot of money which would lead them to their ultimate goal—power. They then could continue on forever, amassing more power. They would never give up.

These shadowy figures were dressed in black from head to toe. They had face masks to hide their identity. Their black boots were perfect for mountain climbing. Their yacht waited below.

It was their escape route. They were after one valuable, the painting, then they would try for the emeralds which they knew were in the National Bank in Munising. They knew everything about Maddie's valuables, and this night with the fierce storm was perfect for them. The storm was the perfect cover which would allow them to get into the keeper's house and to hide their identity. They had been watching the storm formation for days betting on its success of being one of the most fierce storms in the area's history.

As they reached the top of the cliff, they waited until all their colleagues had joined them at the top. Their leader then gave them hand signs to spread out. They were armed and no matter what they had to do, they would get that painting. They even knew about the special security display box and how to handle it. They didn't want to hurt anyone but may have to kill all of them because of one woman who had won the auction in Duluth and taken ownership of the lighthouse.

When the group of men arrived at the keeper's house, they took positions around the house assigned to them by their leader. Three were at the front door with others on both sides of the door. Two stood by the sides of the house, and others were at the back door. Every entrance was covered. They had encircled the whole house. The wind and rain covered any noise they made in surrounding the house.

Inside, Maddie looked at Erick and asked, "Did you hear that sound outside. It was like something hit the house."

"It's probably more falling tree limbs that we'll find tomorrow scattered from here to the cliff, Maddie."

There was a knock on the front door.

"Erick, be careful. Who could that be out in a storm like this?"

Erick turned the light on and slowly opened the door. A man dressed in black was standing with his back to the door.

"Can I help you?"

With that the man swung around.

"You sure can."

The two men on either side of him pushed their way through the door so fast that Erick almost fell backward. Maddie jumped up.

"Who are you and what do you want?"

Two other men followed them in so there were five masked men in their house all brandishing guns.

"We are here, Madame, to get something that belongs to us."

Maddie immediately pushed the alarm which was hidden in her pocket. Erick also pushed his alarm.

"What is it that you want?"

"Well, Madame, I see you have it in a very secure display box hanging on the wall."

"That's my painting", Maddie retorted.

"Unlock that box now!"

"I can't. I don't have the key. It's not in this house", Maddie replied."

"Well, I guess we'll just have to shoot if off the wall."

"If you do that, mister, the box will implode and the painting will be ruined. The box is rigged so that people like you can't get to it. It's the system that most museums use."

"Okay, fair enough. Then both of you sit down. If you, Madame, don't get someone to open it within forty five minutes, your friend, Erick, will die."

He handed Maddie the phone. Maddie dialed Agent Ford's number even though she had already sent her alarm to him.

He answered, "I'm on my way, Maddie. I have the key. I'm about fifteen minutes away. Hang on. They won't hurt you until they get the painting."

As Maddie hung up, she looked at the masked stranger and informed him that the key would be there in fifteen minutes. At the same time, she noticed car lights coming towards her house.

She heard it pull up, then the driver turned off the motor. There was a tap at the door. The masked man opened it, and someone pushed a smaller person into the room. The person was also dressed in black with a full face mask and hood. Behind the person, the Sheriff entered the room. He had his gun out pointing towards the smaller person.

"Oh, Sheriff, I'm so glad you're here. These men are trying to steal my painting."

The Sheriff looked around. The masked men waited for the Sheriff to make a move. Then, the Sheriff spoke, "You guys are getting messy. Look who I found outside."

He pointed to the smaller person who he had pushed through the doorway. Then, he looked at one of the masked men and asked, "Mark, did you know she followed you here? I doubt she would have climbed up that cliff as you did."

Maddie and Erick were shocked. It was apparent that the Sheriff was one of them. Then, Maddie spoke up, "Sheriff, why are you involved with these men?"

"Because, Ms Kirkpatrick, it's very profitable, and it has been going on for a very long time—all the way back to World War II. You see in 1938 Nazi Germany there was a night called 'The Night of Broken Glass.' During that night the Nazis raided the homes of Jewish people who, back then, were very successful and prosperous. They had many valuables that the Nazis stole from their homes. Paintings worth a fortune were taken. Many of these valuables found their way around the world after the war passing from family to family. Many end up in auction houses. You won the auction and received a painting worth a fortune. Our groups find these valuables and sell them for higher prices."

"So, Sheriff, you steal them or take them by force."

"Yes, Ms. Kirkpatrick, we do, but we prefer to win them at auctions or buy them from people who don't know the real value of what they have. So you see, sometimes we do this legally, but other times like your situation, we can't. We do it anyway we can."

The Sheriff then pointed to one of the masked men. You can reveal yourself, Rick. The man took off his mask. Maddie gasped.

"You are that angry man from the Duluth auction who lost the painting to me, and you were also in the bookstore in Sault Ste Marie where you were yelling at the manager."

"You're right, Ms. Kirkpatrick. I was assigned to keep tabs on you. And, now you are going to lose the painting to us."

"Since we're doing some revealing here, I think it is only right if the person who came through the door with me does some revealing. You take off your mask too."

The smaller masked person slowly took off the mask, then burst into tears.

"I'm so sorry, Maddie. I didn't really want to do this."

"Heidi, I can't believe you were involved in this. You are such a good worker at the inn. What would make you do something like this?"

The Sheriff continued, "Heidi you need to introduce your partner."

The masked man next to Heidi took off his mask. This time, Erick gasped.

"It's your boyfriend, Heidi, who would pick you up at the Inn and take you over to Canada for lunch."

"He's not my boyfriend, Erick, he's my husband."

"So, you see", the Sheriff continued, "We even have a little family affair in our group."

Then, Maddie spoke up, "But, Heidi, I met you on the plane from Duluth to Sault Ste. Marie. What a coincidence."

"No, Maddie, it wasn't a coincidence", Heidi added, as she wiped the tears from her face. I was on that plane and my seat was next to you because it was arranged that way after the group learned you had won the lighthouse. My husband and I were at the auction house sitting in the back during the auction. Once you won the painting we or part of the group knew where you were all the time."

Dan Ford had arrived during the revealing conversation taking place in the house. He had parked on the road leading to Glenn's house and walked the rest of the way. He had been informed by his office what he had suspected, that the Sheriff was one of the leaders of the group. He also had information on the rest of the group including Heidi and her husband.

As he walked towards the keeper's house, he saw the masked men standing outside and around the house. He immediately phoned for back up. He took his gun out and decided not to knock but to enter unannounced, and would do it fast before the outside guards saw him.

Stealthily, he approached the door and with no hesitation walked in. He announced, "FBI, put your guns down!" He held up his badge. The Sheriff turned around.

"Well, hello, agent. I was wondering when you would get here with the key."

"Sheriff, put your gun down. I know about your role in the group."

"We have you outnumbered, Agent."

Maddie saw one of the masked men turning his gun on Agent Ford, and before she could warn him, the man shot Agent Ford in the shoulder.

By instinct, Maddie ran over to Dan Ford and knelt down to help him.

"Get back to your seat, Maddie."

"He's bleeding Sheriff. I have to get some towels."

"Make it quick, so we can find the key and get out of here."

The storm had started to quiet down. The claps of thunder were further away. So, when the shot that hit Agent Ford rang out, Glenn heard it from his house. He had been outside with Toby. He knew Erick had a gun but didn't think anyone else was around because of the storm.

"Come on Toby, let's go check on Maddie and Erick."

As they approached the front door of the keeper's house, Glenn didn't notice the guards standing in the shadows. He knocked on the door, and called, "Maddie are you okay?"

Inside, the Sheriff said to Maddie, "go answer the door and get rid of him."

Maddie opened the door only about an inch.

"Maddie, I heard a gun shot coming form your house. Is everything okay?"

In a low voice she answered, "No."

A gust of wind pushed the door further open. Glenn was startled to see the Sheriff.

"Hey, Sheriff, what are you doing here in the middle of this storm?"

Glenn with Toby pushed his way through the door. He saw Agent Ford on the floor, then saw the other masked men.

The Sheriff turned his gun on Glenn.

"Whoa, Sheriff, I'm not the bad guy here."

"No, Glenn, you're not, but you're just the unfortunate guy who saw something he shouldn't, so you've sealed your own fate."

"I think you should think twice about that Sheriff."

The Sheriff cocked his gun as if he were going to shoot Glenn.

In an instant, Glenn yelled, "Toby, go", as he made a hand motion that only Toby understood to mean ATTACK!

With that command, Toby changed from the happy-go-lucky gentle Golden Retriever to an attack dog. Growling, he lunged at the Sheriff knocking his gun out of his hand and holding him down. While the masked men watched in horror as Toby took down the Sheriff, Maddie went over and picked up the gun. She pointed the gun at the masked men.

"Don't ever try to shoot that dog or I will shoot you and Glenn will command Toby to take the rest of you down. Surprise, he is a trained attack dog."

Erick went over to help Agent Ford get his gun out. Ford told Glenn he had called for back up but to also call the State Police. Glenn phoned the State Police and told them to send many police cars as they had just busted a large art smuggling and theft ring in this part of the country.

Maddie could hear the sirens in the distance as they descended on the keeper's house.

There were more police cars then she had ever seen. When they arrived and entered the house, Toby was still standing over the Sheriff. Agent Ford had been able to get up and with Erick's help collect the men's guns.

The masked men who had been standing outside the house ran back to the cliff to scale down to the beach. Maddie had found out that they had arrived by boat, so Erick called the Coast Guard to stop the boat.

As the police handcuffed the men and led them one by one into the waiting police cars, when they led the Sheriff out, he looked back at Maddie and Erick, and ended with, "You may have gotten our group, but we're only a small piece of the organization. Other groups like ours will take over this area."

Then he looked at Toby and said, "I didn't realize you're such a tough fella."

Toby growled goodby and remained alert until the Sheriff was out of sight.

When Glenn, Maddie and Erick were finally alone, Maddie walked over to Toby, petted him gently on his head, then hugged him saying, "You're our hero, Toby. We love you."

Having changed back to his fun loving self, Toby wriggled and nudged his nose into Maddie's hand.

"And, Glenn, if you ever need to go out of town, I would love to take care of Toby for you."

"Thanks, Maddie, that's a deal and I can see that Toby loves you very much."

"And now, you two, I think it is time for Toby and me to go home in order to settle down for the night. It may take some time after a day like today."

"Glenn, you and Toby are more than neighbors to Erick and me, you're part of our family." She hugged Glenn.

CHAPTER 51

Erick and Maddie watched Glenn and Toby slowly walk over the large expansive lawn between their two houses.

"I guess we can finally relax, Erick."

He put his arm around Maddie.

"Yeah, and we still have a lot of work to do. It may be a few months before we are finished and can have our final open house."

Maddie added that she would work on the marketing of their keeper's house and lighthouse.

"Erick, this is such a popular area. I'm going to organize a tourist corner in our house with brochures of all the great things to see on the Shipwreck Coast. I think there should be a brochure shelf between the living room and foyer. We could also have a video showing the beauty of the area. To get my mind off this horrible night, I'm going to start planning the fun.

Maddie started making a mental list of popular tourist attractions. The closest to their B&B was the famous Pictured Rocks National Seashore. You could see it from the backyard of the lighthouse. Brochures had pictures of its magical rock formations. Then there was the abandoned ghost town of Fayette with the remains of the old mining community in near perfect condition. It was also the only cliff area accessible by vehicle which also featured "Lovers Leap,' an arch of rock extended from Pictured Rocks shoreline to an outcrop located in Lake Superior. Then, of course, less than an hour away, there was the famous town of Sault Ste. Marie with its fascinating lock system where tourists could watch freighters from all over the world pass through the locks. There were also state parks with numerous water falls. Then, the most popular of all is the Glass Bottom Shipwreck Tours, an area where Mother Nature caused the majority of shipwrecks, but at the same time she also preserved the remains underneath the water like, as people have described, macabre trophies.

"So, Maddie, who is going to lead these tours?"

"Most of the tours, Erick, have their own leaders, or our guests can visit the local tourism agency in town."

"Well, my dear, I will leave that all up to you as I and the crew have to complete our remodeling tasks."

Maddie smiled and was looking forward to her job. In addition to the tours, she would have fun buying the new furniture for the bedrooms and common areas in both buildings. However, she didn't tell Erick that she still had a fear of the organization the Sheriff had been a part of. He had threatened that even without his leadership, the group would still be in and around the area. She was still worried about the safety of the painting, however, a seed of an idea was forming in her mind of what to do. It would entail more research.

CHAPTER 52

(Six months later)

Maddie and Erick woke up to perfect weather for their final open house. Everything was in place. The new fenced in yard facing Lake Superior was decorated with Spring flowers and balloons.

The difference between this open house and the previous one was that it wasn't open to the public. Maddie and Erick had invited only family and close friends. They insisted that Glenn come since he would be one of their special guests. Brad Elsford and everyone who worked on the remodeling project or associated with it were invited including Bob Wilkins, the architect, Ben, the bookstore owner in Sioux Ste. Marie, Tom Holder, the appraiser, and Mike Thresher, her insurance agent. Carolyn and Doug Hall, Wilson's parents were also invited.

The rooms of the keeper's house and lighthouse had been decorated with furniture and colors which represented the culture of the Shipwreck Coast. The living room in the keeper's house was expertly designed with a conversation area around the fireplace including a sofa, a loveseat, and a couple of cushy chairs. Tables and chairs for four were clustered around the room to be used for the morning breakfast, then as game tables for the rest of the day. An alcove between the kitchen and living room would be used as a self serve breakfast buffet.

The lighthouse had a small bedroom at each level where there was one window in each. There was a small enclosed elevator next to the spiral stairway. All ADA (American Disabilities Act) standards for each building had been applied.

Glenn was the first guest to arrive and although he had seen the progress of the construction through out, Maddie and Erick felt he would always be a part of their family and a very best friend. As he hugged Maddie, Glenn added, "Toby wanted to come but I left him behind to guard the estate, and I needed the freedom of not having to watch a dog."

Maddie told him that Toby was a wonderfully behaved dog, but said she understood.

Carolyn and Doug Hall, Wilson's parents, arrived. Carolyn excitedly said, "Maddie, before I leave I have something important to tell you about my research."

Maddie hugged Wilson and thanked him for his great work with the construction crew.

"So, Wilson, aren't you at the end of your gap year?"

"Yes, Maddie, I'm going back for the next semester."

Maddie hesitated for a moment, then decided to take a chance with a new idea.

"Wilson, I am in the middle of collecting brochures about various tourist destinations and popular places on the Shipwreck Coast, would you be interested in coordinating and helping to be a tour escort for my guests next summer? The pay is good and it would be a fun job. You would also have the assistance of some of the tour escorts in town. Then, in between the various day trips, I would also pay you for odd jobs we will probably have around the lighthouse and the rest of the property such as manning the front desk at the keeper's house."

"That sounds great, Maddie. After being here this year, I feel like the lighthouse is a second home."

"Okay, Wilson, then it's set. As soon as I have my collection of tourist attraction brochures, I will send you a sample of each."

The guests were directed to the backyard of the lighthouse facing Lake Superior. Waiters were circulating through the crowd offering glasses of champagne and other wines. Another server passed a huge tray of the Upper Peninsula speciality—Pasties. There were a variety of fillings. Some were vegetarian, others had a mixture of meats and vegetables.

There were small plates available even though Pasties could easily be finger food. Other finger foods lined silver trays which were placed on beautifully decorated tables sporting Irish linen table cloths and vases filled with flowers of the season.

Music from a string quartet added to the formality of the garden party.

After most of the guests had settled into their conversation groups, one of the waiters set up a small platform near the string quartet and placed a microphone in front of it.

Maddie and Erick stepped up to the platform. Maddie carried a small bell which she rang near the microphone so the guests could hear it above the conversation and the noise of the waves in Lake Superior in the background.

"Thank you all so much for coming to our party as we formally introduce you to the new bed and breakfast on the Shipwreck Coast. Erick and I couldn't have completed this project with out all of you. So, we thank you again for all the talent you brought to our project from the initial architectural design to the fantastic construction work, the legal advice, the interior design advice and to all of the creative ideas. And, especially to the wonderful assistance of my neighbor, Glenn Pedersen, who allowed us to use his lodge for our many meetings and for his kind support through the whole project. He was always there when we needed him. Thanks, Glenn.

Now, there is one more thing that I want to tell you. As you know we almost had our special painting stolen. Our lives were actually in danger for a period of time. That painting is very valuable. We found out that it was stolen from a prominent Jewish family by the Nazis during a raid on their home in 1938. That painting plus other paintings and valuables were stolen from other Jewish families during that time and over the years the paintings have been passed down from generation to generation and from country to country. Most families who were in possession of these valuables had no idea that these were stolen items and never knew the World War II history behind the paintings. So, Erick and I have decided to loan our painting to one of the major Holocaust museums in this country where I am sure it will be safer then hanging in our house. The museum has told me that they will research the painting in hopes of finding the descendants of the family so we could return it to them, however chances are very slim. Once the museum receives the painting, they will contact one of the best artists they know to create a copy of the painting which will then hang in the foyer of our keeper's house here on the Shipwreck Coast."

The crowd clapped and even whistled showing their approval.

Erick then took the microphone and announced, "Maddie and I have a special announcement today. I have asked Maddie to marry me and she has accepted."

Again the crowd broke into a cheer, clapping and whistling. The quartet played "Here Comes The Bride." Then Erick signaled that he had one more announcement.

"This will be the shortest engagement of all times since we have invited the Reverend Martin from Munising to marry us right now."

Reverend Martin stepped out of the crowd and approached the platform. In a matter of minutes and in front of all their friends, Maddie and Erick became husband and wife.

Chapter 53

Maddie and Erick were just finishing brunch after a late night of celebrating their wedding and the completion of the keeper's house and lighthouse bed and breakfast. They were having an enjoyable late start to the day.

The doorbell rang followed by some light knocking. Maddie opened the front door to greet Carolyn and Doug Hall.

"Are you returning home so soon Carolyn? Why don't you come in for some coffee and pound cake?"

Carolyn answered, "We'd love that and I promised to tell you about some new information I found concerning Joey and World War II."

Maddie showed them to the living room and brought in a pot of coffee and a tray of small cakes. Carolyn began the conversation.

"First, Maddie, Wilson told me about your job offer to him for next summer which sounds wonderful and he is so excited. Thank you so much. In fact Doug and I have been talking of looking for a summer rental up here so we could stay for most of the summer and see Wilson and also check out everything there is at the Shipwreck Coast. I'll be checking out those brochures you are sending him about all the tourist attractions. I'm really excited about it."

"Your son has been such a help to us and we've really enjoyed getting to know him. I'm looking forward to seeing him next summer."

"So, what can you tell me about Joey and World War II?"

"As you know, Joey died in Holland during the war in 1945. His superior was a Captain who the soldiers called Captain Sam. We think he used his first name because some of the records we found implied that it was easier and quicker to say than his last name.

I called the Army to see if they could tell me anything about his platoon and about Captain Sam. The Army was very open and helpful. But I finally learned the Captain's full name and it was Samuel Charles Kirkpatrick. Does that ring a bell, Maddie? I understand he was a very kind person but he had high expectations for his soldiers, and was very popular among the men.

Their unit at the time Joey died was like what later would be called a 'Mash Unit' known as a Mobile Army Surgical Hospital. Anyway, Captain Sam was the one who got Joey's letter out of Holland on one of the Great Lakes Freighters that was serving between the Great Lakes Region and Europe. So, it really warmed my heart yesterday when you said you were loaning your painting to a Holocaust Museum because I think you know I am Jewish although Doug is not."

As Maddie listened, she was stunned. She remembered she had been told that her relative with the last name Kirkpatrick had been a Captain in the Army during World War II and was very much revered by her family.

"Carolyn, if you could wait for a few minutes, I may be able to find out some information in some scrapbooks I have. I'll be back right away."

Maddie went to a back closet where there were boxes that needed unpacking. She rapidly looked through them and found one labeled, "Family Stuff from World War II." She brought the scrap book back to the living room.

"Let's look at this together."

They moved to one of the breakfast tables. She turned the pages slowly. Most of the articles were those about specific battles and family members who fought in them. Then, coming to the back of the book, there was a whole page and a half about the battle of Holland. There was a picture of a man who Maddie had been told was her great uncle. His name was Samuel Kirkpatrick. The article referred to him as Captain Sam. There was also a full length picture of him, a strikingly handsome soldier with dark brown hair and a gentle face even though an air of authority surrounded him.

"Wow, Carolyn, this has to be the same man. My grandparents talked about him. He made it home from the war and I heard he was from Michigan. Even though you and I are not related, I almost feel as if we are through this connection."

"Maybe Maddie, we're all a part of a much larger family."

"Yes, Carolyn, I agree, and we should think of it that way. Anyway, we will definitely stay in touch. When or if the museum finds any new connection with anyone or anyplace after its research of the painting, I will definitely let you know. And, I think your relative, Joey, was certainly blessed to have Captain Sam as his superior. Also Captain Sam was blessed to have such a caring soldier as Joey who put his concern for his family's welfare first even when he was dying."

Erick and Doug had silently been listening to the story. As the Halls stood to leave, Erick and Maddie thanked them again, and when she closed the door, as she was turning around, she saw on a shelf beside the door the small model of the lighthouse which was given to her at the auction. Inside there was a spare key to the lighthouse.

She grabbed her camera from a drawer, placed the model lighthouse on a table next to the painting and snapped. She would miss the painting when it was transferred to the museum, but once it was out of her house, the danger would be gone. She was actually looking forward to seeing the copy of the painting, but would have to wait quite a while before it was finished.

Erick put his arm around her as they gazed at the painting.

"We have one more night with the painting. Tomorrow the armored car with two police escorts will come to move it away to the museum. Our worries will be over and we can finally live a normal life and turn off the alarms."

They kissed unaware that they were still being watched from afar.